The Case of the
Cosmic Kidnapping

Startled by what he saw, Joe stepped backward so quickly that he stumbled into Frank. Hovering above the parking lot was a large dome-shaped object. It was about twenty feet across, with a ring of flashing lights that blinked rapidly as it landed.

Suddenly Joe realized that Chet's boss was standing directly underneath the craft. "Mr. Hawkins!" Joe shouted as he ran across the lot. But the dome had already landed and completely swallowed up Mr. Hawkins.

The whining sound grew louder, and the dome began to ascend into the dark sky. Within seconds it had risen about two hundred feet, zoomed over Joe's head, and disappeared.

"Where did it go?" Frank asked, scanning the sky.

"I don't know," Joe said, looking back at the empty parking lot, "but it seems to have taken Chet's boss with it!"

Hardy Boys Mystery Stories

Available from MINSTREL Books

120

The HARDY BOYS®

THE CASE OF THE COSMIC KIDNAPPING

FRANKLIN W. DIXON

A MINSTREL® BOOK

PUBLISHED BY POCKET BOOKS

New York   London   Toronto   Sydney   Tokyo   Singapore

A MINSTREL PAPERBACK *ORIGINAL*

 A Minstrel Book published by
POCKET BOOKS, a division of Simon & Schuster Inc.
1230 Avenue of the Americas, New York, NY 10020

Copyright © 1993 by Simon & Schuster Inc.
Front cover illustration by Daniel Horne

Produced by Mega-Books of New York Inc.

ISBN: 0-671-79310-1

First Minstrel Books printing June 1993

10 9 8 7 6 5 4 3 2 1

Printed in the U.S.A.

Contents

1 Kidnappers from the Sky

"So, Chet, are you sick of hamburgers yet?"

Muscular, blond-haired Joe Hardy, sitting at the counter of a fast-food restaurant, watched Chet Morton through the large serving window. The sight of his husky friend in a chef's apron with a picture of a smiling hamburger on it struck Joe as comical. Chet was flipping a beef patty in the small kitchen of the Happy Burger, the fast-food restaurant where he'd been working for a week as chef and assistant manager.

"Chet sick of burgers?" asked Frank Hardy, who was seated at the counter next to his younger brother. "Are you kidding? That's like asking if the sun rises in the west." Eighteen-year-old

1

Frank was tall and athletic looking, with thick dark hair.

"Come on, guys," Chet said. "Give me a break. Hamburgers are no laughing matter. If I don't keep cooking a constant supply for the crowd, I'll get fired."

Seventeen-year-old Joe looked around the empty restaurant. The "crowd" consisted of him, his brother, Frank's girlfriend, Callie Shaw, and Joe's girlfriend, Iola Morton, who was Chet's sister. All four were seated at the long counter, and they were just finishing their burgers and french fries.

"What crowd?" Joe asked Chet. "If it weren't for us, this place would be dead."

"That's not fair," Iola said. "It's almost nine-thirty, nearly closing time. Everybody's gone home for the night. Right, Chet?" She took a sip of her iced tea.

Chet cast a glum look at his friends. "Well, business actually hasn't been all that good. In fact, you guys are about half the customers we've had all day. If it keeps up like this, this place will close, and I'll lose my job. In fact, the last chef *quit* because he was so bored."

"Well," Callie said, "we'll just have to tell all our friends to come to the Happy Burger."

Joe snorted. "They don't *want* to come here. They're too busy hanging out at Mr. Pizza with everybody else from school. Which is where we'd be if Chet hadn't decided he wanted to get personal with a bunch of beef patties."

"Thanks a lot," Chet said as he slapped the burger he had just cooked between a bun and took a bite of it. "I guess now I know who my real friends are."

"Hey, we're here, aren't we?" Frank said. "As long as you're the chef, we'll spend our evenings at the Happy Burger, scarfing up hamburgers as only Chet Morton knows how to make them."

Callie sighed and picked at her french fries. "Though a pizza *would* taste pretty good about now," she admitted. "Are you sure you can't convince your boss to start selling pizza, too? Maybe it'll improve his business."

"Mr. Hawkins?" Chet asked. "Are you kidding? He's convinced hamburgers are the route to fame and fortune."

A door opened next to the grill, and a young woman appeared wearing an apron with the Happy Burger insignia on it. Louise Kagan was short and slender and wore her dark hair pulled back into a ponytail.

"Mr. Hawkins just finished going over the ledger." She gave Chet a grim look. "And he says you messed it up again."

Chet slapped his hand against the side of his head. "Sorry, Louise. It's that electric calculator he's got back there. I can never remember when to press the plus key."

3

Louise rolled her eyes. "You press it *between* the numbers, Chet!" she said in exasperation.

"Oh, yeah." Chet grinned sheepishly. "I'm sure I'll get it right tonight."

"He asked me to do it tonight, Chet," Louise said. "He wants you to scrub the kitchen until it's spotless. And don't forget the floor."

"Uh-oh!" Joe laughed. "Looks like being an assistant manager may be tougher than you thought."

"Come on, guys." Chet turned toward his friends. "Cleaning is part of the restaurant business."

Chet began scraping the grill with a spatula. He looked through the serving window and gave his friends a sour look. "This is going to take all night," he said, gesturing toward the greasy grill.

Louise's expression softened. "Look, I'll give you a hand with the cleaning, okay? But I've got to finish the ledger first. Otherwise, Mr. Hawkins will be yelling at me, too." She nodded toward the office door.

As if on cue, a man in his late forties stepped through the doorway and into the kitchen. His black mustache was carefully trimmed, and his thick dark hair was slicked back. He wore a navy blue suit with a narrow tie. There was a disapproving look on his face that was directed at Chet.

4

"I see that Louise has already spoken with you, Chet," Fred Hawkins said sternly. "I expect this kitchen to be spick-and-span when I come in tomorrow morning."

"Yes, sir, Mr. Hawkins," Chet said. "The floor will be so clean you can eat off it, sir!"

"Yuck," Joe said under his breath, and Frank made a face.

"Just be sure that the *counter* is so clean you can eat off it," Hawkins said as he came out from the kitchen. He walked around the counter and past the tables that lined one wall of the restaurant. He placed a hand on the door handle, then turned back toward the kitchen. "Oh, Chet?" he said.

Chet snapped to attention. "Yes, Mr. Hawkins?"

"Do you think you could try eating only *five* hamburgers a day?" Then, with a snort, Hawkins opened the door and left.

When the door closed, Chet threw his chef's hat to the floor. "What's with that guy?" he snapped. "He's been ragging on me ever since I came to work here, as though everything that goes wrong is my fault."

"You mean it isn't?" Joe teased.

Iola dug her elbow into Joe's side. "He *was* pretty rough on you," she told her brother. "I mean, even Dad doesn't hassle you that much."

5

"It's not your fault, Chet," Louise said sympathetically. "Mr. Hawkins has been in a bad mood lately."

"Well, it's not my fault he's in a bad mood," Chet said, pacing back and forth behind the counter. "I've really worked hard since I've started. I've even given him some suggestions about increasing business. But did he thank me—"

Suddenly a loud whining sound coming from outside the restaurant cut Chet short. Swiveling on his stool, Joe turned toward the front door. He could hear another sound, too, a low-pitched rumble, like a car engine with a missing cylinder.

"What *is* that noise?" Frank asked, his eyebrows knit together.

"I don't know," Joe said, jumping off his stool. "But I'm going to find out."

He ran to the front door, threw it open, and stepped outside. The Happy Burger was located in a small Bayport shopping center, which consisted of two rows of stores forming a large L around a parking lot. It was nine-thirty, so most of the stores were closed, and the parking lot was almost empty. Except for the light from a few scattered street lamps, the shopping center was dark. In the middle of the lot Joe could just make out Chet's boss, Fred Hawkins. He stood frozen in his tracks, staring up at the night sky.

Joe turned his gaze upward, too. Startled by

6

what he saw, Joe stepped backward so quickly that he stumbled into Frank.

Hovering over the parking lot, about five hundred feet in the air, was a large dome-shaped object! It was about twenty feet across, with a ring of flashing lights that blinked rapidly as the dome descended toward the ground.

"What air force launched that thing?" Frank asked from behind Joe.

Joe glanced over his shoulder. Frank, Callie, Iola, Chet, and Louise were clustered around him, staring up at the sky with their mouths open. When Joe looked back at the apparition, he saw that it was coming in fast for a landing. The whine grew louder, and he covered his ears. As the object touched the ground, a strange wind whistled across the parking lot.

Suddenly Joe realized that Hawkins was still standing directly underneath the descending craft. "Mr. Hawkins!" he shouted. Running across the parking lot, Joe waved his arms, trying to warn the man before it was too late. But the dome clunked to a landing and completely swallowed up Hawkins.

Stunned, Joe slid to a halt. In a second Frank was beside him.

"What's going on?" Frank shouted above the noise.

Joe shook his head. "I don't know. But I don't see Mr. Hawkins."

7

Just then the whining sound grew louder, and the dome began to ascend into the dark sky. Within seconds it had risen about two hundred feet. Then it made a sharp change in course, zoomed over Joe's head, and disappeared over the roof of the Happy Burger.

"Wow!" Joe said as he watched it go. "What was that?"

"And where did it go?" Frank asked, scanning the sky.

"I don't know," Joe said, looking back at the empty parking lot, "but it seems to have taken Chet's boss with it!"

2 Close Encounter

Frank and Joe raced across the parking lot to the spot where Mr. Hawkins had been standing. Frank reached the place first. Crouching down, he picked up a flat wallet, which was visible by the light of one of the street lamps.

Seconds later Chet, Louise, Callie, and Iola joined Frank and Joe. "What happened to Mr. Hawkins?" Louise asked breathlessly.

Frank shook his head. "Your guess is as good as mine. But I just found this," he said, holding out the wallet.

"Does it belong to Mr. Hawkins?" Chet asked.

"Let me see." Frank flipped open the wallet. Behind a clear plastic window was a driver's license. Underneath the picture was the name Frederick W. Hawkins.

"It sure looks like it," Frank said, handing the wallet to Chet. "He must have dropped it."

"That's important evidence," Joe said. "The police will want to see it. And speaking of the police," Joe continued, "someone had better call them."

Callie and Iola volunteered.

"Don't tell them you think you've seen a UFO," Frank called after the girls, who were running back to the restaurant. "They'll think we're all crazy."

"I don't get it," Louise said, her expression puzzled. "One minute Mr. Hawkins was standing here, and the next minute he wasn't!"

"And that's his car over there." Chet pointed to a blue sedan. "So he didn't drive away."

"Then where'd he go?" Joe asked.

"Good question," Frank said. For a minute the teens silently looked around them. There was no way he could have run toward the shops or the street without their seeing him. The only place he could have gone was straight up into the sky.

"He must have had a close encounter," Chet said in a hushed voice.

"Huh?" Joe said. "What are you talking about, Chet?"

"You know," Chet said. "Don't you ever watch science-fiction movies?"

10

Joe shook his head. "I prefer my action a little more down to earth."

"I think Chet's suggesting that that thing we just saw was a UFO," Frank said.

"That's crazy!" Joe scoffed.

"What else could it be?" Chet asked. "You guys saw it. The flashing lights. The whining noise. They don't make airplanes like that. This must be what the flying saucer freaks call a 'close encounter of the third kind.' That's when somebody actually gets taken inside a flying saucer. In this case, my boss!"

Louise put her hands on her hips. "Come on, you guys. There's no such thing as flying saucers."

Frank shook his head in bewilderment. "I don't believe in flying saucers, either," he said. "But that flying object wasn't like any kind of aircraft I've ever seen."

"If it wasn't a flying saucer, how could it have picked up Mr. Hawkins and flown away with him?" Chet asked.

Louise opened her mouth as if to reply, then slowly shut it. "I don't know," she admitted.

"There are lots of things that could have picked Mr. Hawkins up and flown away with him," Joe began. "A helicopter. A hot-air balloon—"

"Did that look like a hot-air balloon to you?" Frank cut in, turning toward his brother. "I've never seen a hot-air balloon make a ninety-degree turn in midair."

11

"And it wasn't a helicopter," Chet said. "It didn't have any blades. And helicopters don't make that kind of whining noise."

Louise shivered. "This is giving me the creeps. First Mr. Hawkins disappears, and now you guys think a flying saucer took him!"

Joe shook his head. "Not me. I don't buy this flying saucer stuff at all."

"Like I said, I don't think flying saucers exist," Frank agreed. "But there are a few respected scientists who *do* believe that there might be intelligent creatures on other planets. And that there's no reason why they couldn't visit earth."

"Well, *I'm* convinced," Chet said. "That was a flying saucer, and it kidnapped Mr. Hawkins! I saw it with my own eyes."

Before anyone could respond, Callie and Iola ran up to them. "Are you guys all right?" Callie asked.

"We're fine," Frank said. "A little confused, but fine."

"Sorry we took so long," Iola said. "But I called Mom and Dad and told them what happened. Of course, they didn't believe me."

Just then a police car, its lights flashing, pulled into the parking lot and drove toward the spot where the group was standing. When the car stopped, a young female police officer leaned out the window on the driver's side.

"We had a report of some sort of disturbance,"

12

she said. "And a possible missing person. Do you know what that's about?"

"You bet we do, officer," Chet said. "We witnessed the whole thing."

The police officer and her partner, a tall, thin man in his thirties, climbed out of the car and quizzed the teenagers about the incident. The female officer took out a notepad and began writing down the details as Chet, Joe, Frank, Louise, Iola, and Callie all tried to tell the story at the same time.

"Whoa," the officer said. "One person at a time."

When it was Chet's turn to describe what had happened, he handed the officer Fred Hawkins's wallet. "And this was all that was left," he told the two officers in a solemn voice.

For a second the police officers looked at each other, then at the teens in disbelief. Then the female officer shrugged, stuck her pad in her pocket, and thanked them. She and the other officer got back into the police car and drove away.

"Do you think she believed us?" Frank asked as they walked back to the Happy Burger. Suddenly a flashbulb went off in his face. When the after-image faded and his vision returned, Frank saw a man standing in front of him with a camera in one hand and a notebook in the other.

"Excuse me," the man said. "I'm Bill Sayres

from the *Bayport Gazette*. Did you say something about a flying saucer?"

"Boy, did we!" Chet declared before Frank could even open his mouth. With excited gestures Chet, Callie, and Iola began telling the reporter the whole story all over again. Louise excused herself to close up the restaurant.

"I'm ready to get out of here," Frank whispered to his brother. "I don't know what happened, but I don't want to be interviewed about some weird flying saucer story."

"You're right," Joe said. "I can just see the headline in the paper tomorrow: 'Wacky Teens See UFO.'"

Frank laughed. "The *Bayport Gazette* isn't exactly one of the scandal tabloids. I don't think the *Gazette* will print a crazy story about flying saucers. If they print anything, it'll probably be a small article on the last page of Section C."

"You may be right," Joe said. "But the disappearance of Fred Hawkins is another thing. Do you think we've got a mystery on our hands?"

Frank nodded. "Exactly the kind of mystery that we ought to be investigating, right?"

"Right," Joe agreed. "After we take Callie and Iola home and get a good night's sleep. Then I'll be ready for anything—even UFOs."

* * *

14

The next morning Frank and Joe awoke to the sound of Aunt Gertrude calling them from the hallway outside their rooms.

"Frank! Joe!" she shouted excitedly. "Guess what? You're in the newspaper."

"Hmmm?" Frank mumbled, stumbling sleepily into the hall. His aunt, a plump and excitable woman who lived with them, handed him the morning's *Bayport Gazette*. Halfway down the front page was a photograph of the Hardys and their friends standing in the parking lot outside of the Happy Burger. Below the photo was the headline: "Was Bayport Visited by Aliens?" The subhead read: "Bayport Businessman Vanishes. Was He Kidnapped by a UFO?"

Rubbing his eyes, Joe came up beside his brother. "Let me see that," he said, snatching the paper from Frank's hands. "Hey, that's us!"

"And our UFO story," Frank added. "Looks as if I was wrong about what the *Gazette* would do with this story. I'm glad Mom and Dad aren't around to see this." Fenton Hardy, a well-known detective, was on a case in Europe and had taken Mrs. Hardy with him. After he finished his assignment, they were going to spend some vacation time in Paris.

"What's this about a flying saucer?" Aunt Gertrude asked them. "This isn't another one of those crazy mysteries you boys get involved with,

15

is it?" Hands on her hips, she glanced back and forth at the two teens.

"Sort of," Frank said, putting his arm around his aunt's shoulders. "And *crazy*'s the right word for it. But don't worry, we'll be careful, as usual."

Aunt Gertrude sighed. "You'd better be. With your parents gone, I feel responsible. Now, breakfast is almost ready, so hurry and get dressed."

When she left, Frank turned back to Joe. His brother was reading the article intently. "I don't believe this," Joe said. "That reporter must have called some experts on UFOs after he talked to Chet, Iola, and Callie."

"He must have woke them up," Frank said, "since it would have been pretty late."

Joe tapped the paper with his finger. "The reporter quotes this guy Hodding Wheatley, who says that earth is being visited by UFOs all the time." He looked at Frank. "Boy, all our friends will be laughing at us now."

"Nah," Frank said. "They'll probably wish they had been there with us."

"Maybe," Joe said. "And once the excitement dies down, we'll probably never hear about it again. But I think we ought to do some investigating to find out what happened to Fred Hawkins." He laughed. "And I was worried about getting *bored* this summer!"

Frank laughed, too. "No way. We've got our

work cut out for us. After breakfast, how about driving over to the Happy Burger?" he suggested, heading back to his bedroom to get dressed. "Who knows? Maybe Fred Hawkins turned up again during the night."

Half an hour later, as the Hardys were eating breakfast, the phone rang. Aunt Gertrude answered it, then gestured to Joe to take it.

"So much for never hearing about that UFO again," Joe said when he'd finished talking.

"Huh?" Frank looked up from his plate of ham and eggs. "Who was that?"

"A reporter from the local TV station, WBPT," Joe said. "She wants to interview us this afternoon at the Happy Burger."

"I'm not sure we should be talking about this," Frank said. "Not if we're investigating Mr. Hawkins's disappearance."

"I agree," Joe said, cutting into his slice of ham. "Anyway, she'd just be disappointed when she hears my theory—that Mr. Hawkins took off for some reason and the UFO was just an elaborate hoax to cover it up."

An hour later Frank and Joe pulled up in front of the Happy Burger in their van. Frank glanced around. The parking lot was surprisingly full, considering that it was only ten o'clock in the morning and the stores had just opened. Parked near the restaurant was a large van painted camouflage green. A sign on the side bore the words UFO Brigade in large letters.

A group of men and women wearing futuristic-looking uniforms made out of shiny silver material stood around the parking lot. On the front of their flight jackets, they wore silver pins shaped like flying saucers. One of the guys in the group turned and gave the Hardys a suspicious look as they got out of their van.

"Who are these guys?" Joe asked. "They look like they got off at the wrong galaxy."

"I don't know," Frank said. "But I don't think they're waiting for Chet's burgers."

As Frank and Joe walked toward the restaurant, one of the men approached them. He was in his mid-forties, heavyset, with thick black eyebrows and a broad face covered with whisker stubble. He stared at Frank and Joe belligerently. "I've seen you fellows before," he said, poking his finger in Frank's face.

Frank pushed the guy's hand away. "What are you talking about?"

The man squinted, then nodded. "Now I know where I've seen you. You were on the cover of the Bayport newspaper." He turned to the men behind him. "Hey! These are the teenagers that had the sighting last night!"

"Uh-oh," Joe whispered in Frank's ear. "I bet these guys are a bunch of UFO freaks. We'd

18

better make a run for the restaurant before they start asking for autographs."

But turning back to Frank and Joe, the man started barking out commands like a marine drill sergeant. "Tell us everything that you saw. Everything! Now!"

"Hey, listen," Frank said in a calm but firm voice, "we were just stopping off at the Happy Burger to see a friend. We'll talk to you later, okay?"

Cocking an eyebrow, the man stepped closer. "Why can't you talk with me now? Are you trying to cover something up?"

"Hey! Lay off," Joe snapped. Nudging Frank aside, he confronted the man in the silver suit. "We don't have to tell you anything."

"We'll see about that!" the man retorted, pushing up his sleeves.

Just then a redheaded man also wearing a silver suit walked up and put his hand on the heavyset man's shoulder. "Hey, Carl. Go easy on these kids, okay?"

Carl Thurmon shrugged off the other man's hand. "Why should I?" he asked. "They had the sighting. We need to talk to them before the government goons get hold of them and hush it all up."

Joe snorted. "I'll talk to the 'government goons' before I'd talk to *you!*"

"Just like I thought." Raising a clenched fist, Carl Thurmon grabbed Joe's shirt.

Joe gripped the man's wrist and swiftly wrenched it so that the man had to let go of the shirt.

Thurmon glared menacingly at Joe, who looked back coolly. "It's my duty to make sure you never get the chance to talk to the government," Thurmon growled, "or anyone else!"

3 Saucer Mania

Frank stepped between Joe and Thurmon, ready to defend his brother if necessary.

"Thurmon!" a voice barked as two men grabbed Thurmon's arms and pinned them behind his back.

Immediately, Joe dropped his fists. "What's this guy's problem?" Joe asked the group as he looked disdainfully at the heavyset man.

With a growl Carl Thurmon lunged toward Joe, but the men held him fast.

"Cut it out, Carl!" the redhead ordered. "We don't need any trouble here."

Frank put a restraining hand on Joe's arm. "Neither do we," he told his brother.

21

"Yeah, okay," Joe said, turning to Frank. "Come on. Let's go see Chet."

"Wait a minute," the redhead said as the other two men led Thurmon away. He stuck out his hand. "I'm Dan Hoffman, head of the local branch of Brigaders. I apologize for Carl. He's a bit of a hothead, and we sometimes have trouble keeping him under control."

"A *bit* of a hothead?" Joe said, gesturing at the man's departing back. "I'd suggest a muzzle for a guy like that."

"We accept your apology," Frank said. Then he glanced at the van. "So you guys are the UFO Brigade?"

"That's correct," the man said.

"What exactly do you do?" Joe asked.

Dan Hoffman spoke with obvious enthusiasm. "The Brigade is an organization dedicated to finding out the truth about unidentified flying objects."

"What have you found out so far?" Joe asked, raising one eyebrow. "That it's all a big hoax?"

Hoffman looked at Joe with piercing green eyes. "It's not a hoax. We believe that UFOs are actual attempts by an alien race to contact humanity. It's the Brigade's mission to find out what the aliens have to say and bring that message to our fellow human beings."

Joe rolled his eyes.

"If these aliens are so anxious to contact us," Frank asked, "why haven't they done it yet?"

"They have," the Brigader said. "Many times. But it's in the interest of powerful individuals in our government to keep the information secret."

Frank shook his head. "So that's what that Thurmon guy was ranting about. It's hard to believe the government would be involved with UFO investigations."

"Let's face it," Joe cut in. "It's hard to believe any of this stuff, period!"

A dark veil fell over Dan Hoffman's eyes. "Suit yourself. But you'll be surprised when the aliens' message finally arrives. Perhaps today will turn out to be the time."

"How did the Brigade get here so fast?" Frank asked.

"We monitor newspapers all over the United States, looking for stories on UFO sightings," the man said. "One of our members who lives in this area saw the story in the *Bayport Gazette* at five-thirty this morning. A general alert went out across the country to our membership, who are converging on Bayport at this moment."

"You mean there're more of you to come?" Joe exclaimed. "I hope there aren't any more like Mr. Thurmon."

"There's nobody quite like Mr. Thurmon," the Brigader said, a hint of a smile on his lips.

Frank thanked the UFO Brigader for giving them the information, then motioned Joe into the Happy Burger.

To Frank's surprise, the place was packed. Chet waved at them from the grill, where he was cooking four beef patties at a time. Louise was racing around serving customers soft drinks and coffee while they waited for their hamburgers and fries.

"Hi, guys!" Chet called through the serving window. "Guess what? Business is great!"

Two people at the counter had just stood up, and Frank and Joe quickly took their places. "So we noticed," Frank said as he slid onto a stool. "What happened? Did Mr. Pizza close down?"

"Nah," Chet told him. "It's the flying saucer story in the paper this morning. Everybody's coming over here to get a look at the spot where the UFO landed. We decided to open early so when they get hungry, they can come in here. It's been like this since eight o'clock this morning. It would be even better if those UFO Brigaders weren't out there scaring half the customers away."

"Hamburgers for breakfast," Joe said with a grimace. "Just what I always wanted."

"What about your boss?" Frank asked. "Did he ever show up again?"

Chet frowned. "No," he said, shaking his head. "He's still missing. I'm starting to get worried. Not that I actually miss him, but he *does* write my paycheck."

Louise looked up from filling a soda. "Don't let Chet fool you," she told Frank. "He's as worried about Mr. Hawkins as I am. I mean, Fred wasn't really that bad a guy. And when I talked to his wife, Clarissa, this morning, she was frantic. People aren't supposed to just vanish like that— into thin air."

"Uh-oh." Chet nodded toward the front door. "More hungry tourists."

Turning, Frank saw a man and woman walk in. The man had a camera around his neck. Immediately he began snapping pictures of the restaurant. The woman glanced excitedly around the area as she made her way toward the Hardys.

"Is this the place where Fred Hawkins worked?" she asked, leaning across the counter.

"Yes, it is, ma'am," Chet said, continuing to cook hamburgers.

"Er, did you know Mr. Hawkins?" Joe asked her.

"Oh, no," the woman said. "We just read about him in the newspaper. It's so exciting! A man kidnapped by a UFO right here in Bayport!"

"Things like that don't happen very often," the man with the camera said. "So we figured we'd come down here and take some pictures of the place where it happened. Someday we may want to show them to our grandchildren."

25

"You don't mind if we take a look around?" the woman asked Chet.

"No, ma'am," Chet said. "Then have a seat. A table should be opening up soon. We make the best burgers in town."

Joe rolled his eyes. "I can't believe this is happening."

"I don't mind," Chet said, slapping three more patties on the grill. "I bet they order a couple of hamburgers before they leave."

"Listen," Frank said to Chet, "Joe and I want to investigate Fred Hawkins's disappearance. We're both skeptical about the UFO kidnapping story. Do you think we can talk to his wife?"

There was a jingling noise as the front door opened again. Chet looked up. "Why don't you ask her?" he replied. "She just came in."

Frank turned to see an attractive, middle-aged woman come through the doorway. She was tall and slender, with a halo of carefully groomed blond hair. She wore a flower-splashed summer dress and sandals, but there was a worried expression on her face, and her red-rimmed eyes told Frank she'd been crying.

She stepped up to the counter. "Has there been any word from Fred since you called me last night?" she asked Chet, her voice trembling. "He hasn't phoned or tried to get in contact in any way, has he?"

Chet shook his head. "Sorry, Mrs. Hawkins.

And believe me, if we hear anything, you'll be the first person we call."

"Excuse me, Mrs. Hawkins." Frank stood up and held out his hand. "I'm Frank Hardy. Could my brother and I speak to you for a minute?"

"I'm sorry," Mrs. Hawkins said distractedly as she dabbed at her swollen eyes with a wadded-up tissue. "If I've met you before I—I don't recall."

"We're Frank and Joe Hardy, ma'am," Joe said gently. "We were here last night when your husband, er, disappeared."

She looked at the Hardys with new interest. "Oh, that's right," she said. "I saw your pictures in the paper this morning. I thought your names sounded familiar. Haven't you . . . helped the police out in the past?"

"Yes," Frank said. "We're detectives."

"Oh." Mrs. Hawkins gasped, and she sat down on the stool Frank offered her. He thought she was about to break out crying again. "I—I suppose it's too much to ask that you might help search for my husband?"

"That's what we wanted to ask you about," Frank replied. "We'd like to help in any way we can."

Mrs. Hawkins sighed. "I'd like that. The police not only seem baffled, but I feel as if they're laughing at me. I think they've decided that Fred just took off and rigged the UFO thing as a distraction."

27

"Why don't we sit at a table by the window?" Frank suggested, gesturing to one that had just emptied. "It'll be more private."

When the three were settled, Mrs. Hawkins leaned over the table toward Joe and Frank.

"I'll answer any questions if it will help," she said eagerly. "My name is Clarissa Hawkins. Fred and I have been married for—what is it now?—twenty-two years. This is the first time in all that period that we've been apart." She closed her eyes for a moment and dabbed at them with the tissue.

"That was actually our first question," Joe said. "Mr. Hawkins has never disappeared like this before?"

Mrs. Hawkins shook her head. She spoke crisply, as if trying to keep her voice from shaking. "Never. Even when he was going to be gone for a few hours, he would call to let me know where he was and how late he'd be."

"So he didn't say anything about leaving town?" Frank asked.

"No," Mrs. Hawkins said firmly. "Definitely not. That's why I'm so worried!" She looked at the Hardys with tear-filled eyes. "You two boys were there when he—when he disappeared. Was he really taken away in some kind of UFO, like it said in the paper?"

"Well . . ." Joe hesitated. "It sure looked that

28

way. This dome-shaped flying object landed in the middle of the parking lot. And the next thing we knew, Mr. Hawkins was gone."

Mrs. Hawkins shook her head in disbelief. "The newspaper said that it was a UFO. Surely that isn't possible."

"We're not sure what's going on," Frank said. "That's why we want to investigate."

"Thank you," Mrs. Hawkins said, relief flooding her face.

"Is it possible that someone might have had a motive for kidnapping your husband?" Joe asked.

Mrs. Hawkins hesitated. "I'm not sure," she finally said. "I wish I could tell you that nobody did, but lately Fred has been acting strange. You know, he looks over his shoulder a lot, as if somebody might be following him. And there have been several phone calls in the middle of the night, though he's never told me who they're from."

"Do you have any idea who's been calling?" Frank asked. "And what he's worried about?"

"No," Mrs. Hawkins told him. "But if I think of anything, I'll let you know. And if you find anything at all that might explain Fred's disappearance, *please* contact me immediately."

"We will," Joe said seriously.

Mrs. Hawkins shook hands with Frank and Joe, then stood up to find Louise.

At that moment a camera crew burst through the door. The name WBPT-TV was emblazoned on their equipment.

"Uh-oh," Joe whispered to his brother. "Do we really want to talk to these guys right now?"

Frank shook his head. "We can talk to the reporters this afternoon, if we have to. Right now we've got to start looking for evidence."

The Hardys got up from the table and started for the door. But they stopped in their tracks when a loud voice boomed into the restaurant from outside.

"We have come from the planet Zondoz!" the voice declared in deep, resonant tones. "We've kidnapped Fred Hawkins, and we have now returned for you, Earthlings!"

4 Tiny UFOs

"Oh, great. It sounds as if the alien kidnappers are coming back for more," Joe said in mock disgust.

"Quit being funny," Frank replied, starting for the front door. "Let's take a look. This just might have something to do with Mr. Hawkins's disappearance."

Frank led the way past the tables of startled customers and threw open the door to the Happy Burger. A huge crowd had gathered in the parking lot, and people were coming out of the stores in the shopping center. In the middle of the lot, in the same spot where Fred Hawkins had vanished the night before, was a large truck with a pair of loudspeakers on the top. On the side of the truck were the words WBBX: Where Bayport Comes to Rock!

"Oh, no." Joe groaned. "Not WBBX! I used to work for those guys."

"What do they think they're up to?" Frank asked. "Some sort of practical joke?"

"We come in peace, Earthlings!" the voice from inside the truck announced. "All we want is a few laboratory specimens so we can take them apart and see what makes them tick!"

"It sounds like a typical WBBX joke to me," Joe said, taking off across the parking lot. When he reached the truck, he knocked on the door. A moment later the door opened and a scowling technician, wearing a WBBX T-shirt and a pair of headphones, looked out. "Yeah, what do you want?"

"What do you guys think you're doing?" Joe demanded, trying to hide a smile. "We've got enough trouble around here already."

From behind the technician a blond-haired disc jockey looked out at Joe. "Oh, it's you, Hardy. He used to work at the station," he told the technician. "How're you doing, Joe?"

"Fine, Mike," Joe said, "until you jokers came along."

Mike laughed. "Chill out, Joe. We're doing a remote broadcast from the shopping center. This is the hottest place in town right now, so we thought we'd generate a little fun, get people worked up."

"Well, go generate it someplace else," Joe said. "Fred Hawkins's kidnapping is serious business. He's really missing."

"Snatched by little green men from outer space?" Mike chuckled. "Yeah, sure. I'm a Martian myself on my mother's side."

"Very funny," Joe said. "Only do me a favor and keep the jokes to yourself."

"Okay, okay," Mike said as the technician slid the door closed in Joe's face.

Frank came up behind his brother. "Sounds as if you let him have it."

"He could use it," Joe said. "That guy Mike's a jerk. When I had that show on WBBX, he was always switching my tape cartridges when I wasn't looking."

Frank glanced around the parking lot. "Have you noticed how many people are here now?"

Joe followed Frank's gaze. When they had arrived less than an hour earlier, the parking lot was quite full for ten o'clock in the morning. But now it was packed. People were standing among the parked cars and milling along the sidewalk. Storeowners had set up sidewalk sales to take advantage of the crowd. Some of the gawkers were taking pictures, others were simply staring into the sky. And the word *UFO* seemed to be on everybody's lips.

"Wow!" Joe exclaimed. "It looks as if we've created a tourist attraction. And I see more Brigaders have shown up, too." He pointed to another van parked next to the first one. "They must have heard about the UFO on WBBX."

"It's on all the radio stations, fella," said a man who was passing by at that moment. "And TV, too. This is the hottest story in town."

Frank shook his head. "And I thought it would be buried in the back of the paper." Suddenly Frank snapped his fingers. "That's it!" He turned to Joe. "Did you notice how much more business there is at the Happy Burger than last night?"

"Sure," Joe said. "You'd have to be blind to miss it. The place is packed."

"And all of those people are here because they heard about Fred Hawkins getting kidnapped by a flying saucer," Frank continued thoughtfully.

Joe's eyes widened. "You're right! And Chet was just saying how bad business has been. You think his boss did all this just to get publicity for the restaurant?"

Frank frowned. "I don't know. It seems kind of drastic. And wouldn't he have let his wife in on his scheme?"

"It's Frank and Joe!" someone shouted before Joe could answer. He turned to see Callie and Iola, standing with a group of their friends. Callie waved to them. "Come on over!"

The Hardys walked toward the group. Iola was

34

chatting with four girls Joe recognized from school. He could tell by the rapt expressions on their faces that they were absorbing everything Iola was telling them.

As he got closer, Joe could hear what Iola was saying.

"And when this—this flying saucer thing took off," Iola said, "Mr. Hawkins was completely gone. Disappeared!"

"Amazing!" one of the girls gasped. "And you never saw him again?"

Iola shook her head. "It was as if he had never been there."

"Except for his wallet lying on the ground," Callie chimed in. "Frank was the one who found it," she added, grabbing Frank by the arm.

"That's so exciting!" one of the girls exclaimed. "I wish I'd been there."

"Tell them what you found when you got to the middle of the parking lot," Iola said to Frank and Joe. "Were there any strange vibrations in the air? Was the ground still hot where the flying saucer had been?"

Frank thought Iola was getting a little carried away, but he decided not to say anything about it. "No," he answered calmly. "No vibrations. No heat. In fact, we didn't find much of anything." He shrugged. "Except the wallet."

"That's no fun," one of the girls said. "Surely you must have found *something* interesting."

35

"Nope," Joe said quickly. Grabbing Frank's other arm, he pulled him away from Callie. "My brother and I were just heading back into the restaurant to talk with Chet. Weren't we, Frank?"

"That's right." Frank nodded emphatically. "We've got to keep investigating this case."

"You're investigating the disappearance of Fred Hawkins?" another of the girls exclaimed. "Now, *that's* exciting!"

"Right," Joe said. "Well, see you later."

With a wave, Joe and Frank headed back to the Happy Burger as rapidly as they could make their way through the crowd.

"Whew. That was a close one," Joe said. "People are really going nuts over this story."

When they entered the restaurant, they found that Chet Morton had come out from the kitchen and was talking with a reporter from WBPT-TV. Chet was telling her all about working at the Happy Burger and how Mr. Hawkins had given him the most important job of his career. There seemed to be no escape from that reporter, Frank thought. He looked at Joe and nodded toward the door. The two boys did an immediate U-turn and headed back into the parking lot.

"Now what?" Joe said.

"If we're going to decide whether Fred Hawkins was really kidnapped by aliens, maybe it's time we learned a thing or two about UFOs," Frank said, pointing to a bookstore on the other side of the shopping center. "They ought to have a few books on UFOs. Let's take a look."

When they reached the store, Frank asked at the front counter where they could find books on UFOlogy. The clerk directed them toward a shelf, but most of the books on flying saucers were already gone—apparently the morning's crowd of people had had the same idea as the Hardys. But Frank found a shop-worn copy of a book called *Visitors from Beyond,* by an author named Hodding Wheatley. He took it to the front counter and paid for it.

When he looked around for Joe, he found his brother in the comic book section.

"What did you find?" Frank asked.

Joe held up the cover of the comic book he was looking through. *"Mutants from Outer Space,"* he read.

Frank had to chuckle. "Looks real factual," he said. "Let's pay for it and head to the van. It'll be the most private place around."

About half an hour later Joe put down his comic book and looked at the cover of the book Frank was reading. "The guy who wrote that book is the same one they quoted in the paper this morning, right?" he asked Frank.

"Yeah," Frank said. "Hodding Wheatley—what a weird name. But it fits him because he writes some weird stuff. He claims that he's been on board a UFO. Only he calls it a lifeship."

37

Joe frowned. "Sounds like Wheatley's been staring at his word processor too long."

"Not only that," Frank said as he quickly thumbed through the pages, "but he says there are whole groups of people who claim to have been kidnapped by alien beings. He belongs to one of these groups himself."

"Sort of UFO Nuts Anonymous?" Joe joked.

Frank chuckled. "Yep. But who knows? Maybe he's telling the truth."

"I'll believe that when I get invited inside a UFO myself," Joe replied. "So what does this Wheatley guy say these aliens did to him?"

"They sort of poked and prodded him," Frank said. "Like they were examining him." Frank frowned. "He also mentions that stuff about the government covering up UFO sightings, like that Brigader was telling us."

"Do you suppose Wheatley belongs to the Brigade?" Joe asked.

"I don't think so," Frank said. "He doesn't sound like the type. But he does say that the government has some sort of top-secret organization called the UFO Working Committee that investigates sightings of unidentified flying objects. And there are lots of people who believe that there are some major sightings the committee may be covering up."

"Why would the government do that?" Joe asked.

"I haven't gotten that far," Frank said. "Maybe we should ask those UFO Brigaders." He nodded toward the group milling around the two vans. "We need to check them out, anyway."

"Good idea," Joe said, taking the book from Frank. "I'll hang on to this in case we need to check out some facts later." He opened the door and stepped out of the van.

Frank got out on his side. Suddenly there was a whistling noise, and Frank looked up to see a small disk-shaped object zooming through the air across the parking lot.

It was heading directly toward Joe!

5 Attack of the Brigader

"Look out!" Frank cried. "Incoming at six o'clock!"

Joe spun around just in time to see the flying object come whizzing toward his face. Reacting quickly, he raised the book that he held in his hand.

The disk barely slowed as it hit the book's cover and ricocheted off. Joe watched it make a wide circle above the heads of several bystanders, then swing straight back toward him. This time he grabbed the door of the van and yanked it open, then ducked behind it.

The flying object hit the metal part of the door with a bang, then fell to the ground. Stooping down, Joe tucked the book under his arm and picked up the object. It was shaped like a flying saucer, about twelve inches across. When he tapped the dome-shaped top, he decided it was made of hard plastic.

"Good moves!" Frank told his brother as he came around the front of the van. "If that thing had hit you, it would have put a huge dent in your head."

"Yeah," Joe agreed. "And I'd have had all those UFO people poking and prodding *me*." He rolled his eyes in disgust.

"What *is* that thing, anyway?" Frank asked. "Was it actually flying under its own power—or is it just some kind of super Frisbee?"

Joe turned the saucer over. He saw a cylindrical object about the size of a small soda bottle recessed under the dome.

"It's self-propelled," Joe said, handing the saucer to Frank. "This cylinder looks like the ones I've seen on those model rockets you buy in hobby stores."

Suddenly Carl Thurmon appeared from out of the crowd. "Hey!" the Brigader said, noticing the Frisbee-shaped object in Joe's hands. "What are you doing with my UFO?"

"I should have known that you'd be behind this!" Joe snapped at the man.

Carl Thurmon locked Joe in his steely gaze. "Behind what?"

41

"You just about took off my brother's head with your little toy," Frank replied.

"That was an accident," Thurmon said, but Joe could tell by the smirk on the man's face that he had intended Joe to be his target.

"That's only a model," Carl Thurmon continued. "I keep it around for demonstration purposes. It can do some impressive loop-de-loops, but it couldn't hurt anyone. Unless he was a wimp," he added with a nasty chuckle.

"Easy, Joe." Standing behind Joe, Frank put his hand on his brother's arm. "He's trying to goad you into taking the first punch."

For a long moment Thurmon glared at Joe. Then he shrugged, grabbed the saucer, and walked into the crowd.

"What do you think that was all about?" Frank asked when the man was gone.

"I'd say that guy's out to get me," Joe said.

"What's he got against you?" Frank said.

"I guess he's still angry about that run-in we had earlier," Joe explained. "He strikes me as the sort who holds a grudge . . . forever."

"Or maybe he really *does* suspect we're government agents." Frank chuckled. "Disguised as teenagers."

"Do you think that he was acting on his own or that the rest of the UFO freaks were behind that little incident?" Joe asked as he slammed the van door.

As if on cue, Dan Hoffman, the red-haired Brigader, strode up to the Hardys. "Was Carl bothering you again?" he asked.

"Yeah, he and his little toy," Frank said.

The Brigader frowned. "I hope there weren't any problems."

"Nothing that some quick reflexes didn't solve," Joe said angrily.

"What's the matter with that guy, anyway?" Frank asked the Brigader.

Dan Hoffman hesitated. "Mr. Thurmon had a bad experience years ago, before he was in the Brigade," he finally answered. "It seems to have warped his outlook on life. He thinks everybody's out to stop him from learning the truth about UFOs. Sometimes he doesn't even seem to trust his fellow Brigaders."

"Why do you keep him around?" Joe asked.

Hoffman shrugged. "What makes you think we have a choice? Besides, we figure it's better to have him as a member, so we can keep an eye on him. If we weren't there to keep him under control, he'd probably do things that would give all UFO enthusiasts a bad name. And that would hurt the Brigade."

"Makes sense," Frank said. Then he looked at the Brigader with interest. "Have you ever heard of a guy named Hodding Wheatley?" He pointed to the book under Joe's arm.

The Brigader's face lit up. "Of course. Mr.

Wheatley is a true believer in UFOs. He's had several sightings himself."

"Then why didn't the government cover *him* up?" Joe asked.

"Because Wheatley didn't have any physical proof that he'd actually been in contact with aliens," the Brigader explained.

"You really believe in this government conspiracy, huh?" Joe eyed the Brigader.

"Of course," Hoffman said with a smile. "We have reports indicating the government has had communication with aliens. They have never been officially revealed because the top brass in Washington doesn't want the public to think they're crazy."

"That's assuming that aliens exist to communicate with," Frank said.

The Brigader raised his eyebrows. "So you still aren't a believer even after you saw a UFO yourself?"

Frank shrugged. "We haven't proved that it was a real one yet."

"That's what the Brigaders are here to do," Dan Hoffman said with great seriousness. "When we find conclusive evidence that there was a UFO here last night, perhaps the world will finally listen to us." He nodded to the Hardys. "Now, if you'll excuse me, I have to go."

Hoffman melted back into the crowd. Joe and Frank exchanged dubious glances.

"So what do you think?" Frank asked his brother.

"I think it's lunchtime," Joe said. "And that I could handle a big, juicy cheeseburger now. I also think we'll find our answers to Fred Hawkins's disappearance at the Happy Burger."

They started across the parking lot.

"What do you think we'll find at the restaurant?" Frank asked.

Joe paused before opening the door of the Happy Burger. "I'm not positive," he said. "But I think if we snoop around Hawkins's office, we may find the *real* reason why he vanished."

Frank and Joe wandered about the restaurant for a moment, trying to find a place to sit. It was now even more crowded than it had been earlier. Chet and Louise were working frantically to make enough hamburgers and fries. When the Hardys finally grabbed a table, Louise barely glanced at them as she hurriedly handed them menus.

After lunch Frank went into the kitchen to talk with Chet, but his friend was almost too busy flipping hamburgers to say much.

"Chet, can you tell me anything more than you did last night about how Fred Hawkins's business has been doing lately?" Frank asked.

"Not really," Chet said as he lined up five hamburger patties on the grill. "I don't really

45

know much about the business end of things here."

"But you're the assistant manager," Frank said.

"True," Chet said. "But I'm still learning. Remember, I just started. And I don't understand the double-entry ledger at all. Maybe you'd better ask Louise."

Frank looked around. Louise looked frantic as she rushed from customer to customer.

"Louise seems to be busy," he said. "How about if Joe and I take a look in the office on our own? We're hunting for anything that can help us find your boss."

"Sure," Chet said, waving to the door beside him. "Just don't take anything."

"Thanks!" Frank said, clapping Chet on the shoulder. Then he waved to Joe, who was paying the check.

After entering Mr. Hawkins's office, the Hardys carefully closed the door behind them and looked around. Frank wanted to see the ledger, which was sitting right in the middle of a large, cluttered desk. It was open to a page with the current date on top of it.

"I'll check out his accounts," Frank said, pulling up a black imitation-leather swivel chair.

Joe headed toward a file cabinet. "Maybe I'll see what Hawkins has stashed in here."

"Good idea," Frank said as he sat down at the

46

desk. Leaning over the ledger, he flipped back through the last several pages. The thing that immediately caught his eye was that it was full of red ink. As far back as he could flip, many of the numbers in the far right column of the ledger were red.

Red ink meant only one thing: debt. Fred Hawkins was running his restaurant in the negative column. Of course, that wasn't unusual for a business venture that was only six months old, but the numbers in red were large. When Frank totaled them up, it appeared that Hawkins was thousands of dollars in debt.

A whistle from the other side of the room made Frank look up. "What did you find?" he asked his brother.

Joe held up a folder labeled Loans. "Looks as if Hawkins borrowed big from some guy named William Harbison."

"That verifies what I discovered," Frank said as he stood up. "Fred Hawkins was in debt up to his eyeballs. I wouldn't be surprised if Harbison turns out to be a loan shark. He probably loaned Hawkins the money with outrageous interest rates, and now Hawkins can't pay up."

Joe carefully replaced the file in the cabinet, then shut the drawer. "I just bet all we have to do is find this William Harbison dude," he said, "and he'll tell us why Fred Hawkins disappeared."

Frank frowned. "You think Fred's on the run because he owes Harbison money?"

"Right on, brother," Joe said, grinning. "Probably Harbison is looking for him, too."

"Unless . . ." Frank's voice trailed off as another thought crossed his mind. "Unless Harbison already found Fred Hawkins last night in the parking lot."

Joe's grin faded. "What do you mean?"

"Maybe the UFO wasn't covering up Fred's disappearance," Frank said grimly. "Maybe it was covering up his murder!"

6 The Man Who Talked with Aliens

"Murdered!" a voice cried out behind Joe. "Fred Hawkins was *murdered*?"

Joe spun around. He hadn't heard the door open. Louise was standing frozen in the office doorway. Her mouth had dropped open, and her eyes were wide with shock.

"Uh, no, Louise. We don't know that Fred was murdered," Frank explained quickly. "It's just that Joe and I found out your boss owes some guy big bucks."

Louise moaned. "Oh, no, just wait until Mrs. Hawkins hears about this."

Joe waved both hands in the air. "Don't tell Mrs. Hawkins until Frank and I know for sure what happened. You'll only upset her."

"You're right," Louise agreed, pushing her dark hair out of her eyes. "And by the way, some reporter's looking for you."

Joe and Frank groaned in unison as they followed Louise out of the office. "I knew that reporter would catch up with us eventually," Frank said. "Let's make it quick."

They were making their way through the crowd when Joe overheard one of the TV crew members mention the name Hodding Wheatley.

Turning to Frank, Joe said, "You know, I bet we're going to get pretty sick of this Hodding Wheatley guy over the next few days. I mean, who cares about some crackpot who believes he was kidnapped by a UFO?"

"Pardon me?" a voice said from behind Joe's shoulder.

Joe turned to see a middle-aged man with distinguished gray hair and a pale complexion who was wearing a tailored suit and silk tie. He was looking at Joe with an expression of amusement.

"Yes?" Joe said. "Do I know you?"

"Apparently you know *of* me," the man said. "I'm Hodding Wheatley."

Joe's face reddened. "I really didn't mean to . . . you know."

Wheatley laughed. "Yes, I understand. I'm quite used to people making fun of my experiences."

Frank chuckled. "My brother sticks his foot in his mouth a lot, Mr. Wheatley."

"I take it that you two are the brothers who had something to do with the UFO sighting last night." He pulled out a newspaper that he was carrying under one arm and held up the front page. It was the *Bayport Gazette*.

"Yep. That's us." Joe rolled his eyes. "I hope you don't mind my saying so, but we don't really believe any of that stuff about an alien kidnapping Mr. Hawkins."

"Though according to your book, kidnappings like this happen all the time," Frank said.

"Well, yes," Mr. Wheatley said, with a hint of a smile. "But they don't usually happen so publicly. That's the problem with UFO kidnappings. There's rarely any evidence left behind or any witnesses other than those who were fortunate enough—or unfortunate enough, depending on your viewpoint—to be kidnapped. That's what makes the Bayport incident so interesting. There were witnesses like you two who can describe it in detail."

"What about your own kidnapping?" Joe asked. "Aren't you a credible witness?"

Mr. Wheatley shrugged. "Not according to some people. They believe I made up the whole story to sell a lot of books and get rich. Or they think the whole thing was in my head. And

51

perhaps there's just a touch of truth behind that accusation."

Frank frowned. "But you said in the book—"

"Excuse me," said a feminine voice from behind Wheatley. Joe looked around the author to see a stylish woman with stiff blond hair and a frozen grin on her glamorous face. He recognized her as the reporter from WBPT-TV. But she wasn't interested in the Hardys. She was staring at Hodding Wheatley instead.

"Did I hear you say that you are Hodding Wheatley?" she asked.

"Indeed I am," Wheatley said. "I'm afraid I haven't had the pleasure . . ."

"I'm Gloria Forbin, from WBPT-TV," the reporter said, extending her hand. "I'd really appreciate it if you could give us an interview concerning this UFO business."

"I'd be pleased," Wheatley said. "I just drove here from New York City this morning in case someone wanted to make use of my expertise."

The reporter linked her arm through his. "That's exactly what we'd like to do," she said, leading Wheatley in front of the camera.

"Maybe we're off the hook," Joe said to Frank.

The Hardys watched as Wheatley stood in the sharp glare of two portable spotlights. Gloria Forbin asked the author to identify himself, then asked him a few other simple questions. Finally she urged him to tell the story of his kidnapping.

"I was lying in bed one evening after my wife had gone to sleep," Wheatley said in a soft yet powerful voice that Joe found mesmerizing. "My mind was full of ideas about what I was going to write the next day, and then a strange sense of peace fell over the room."

"Isn't it usually peaceful and quiet at night?" Ms. Forbin cut in.

"Not necessarily," Wheatley said. "We were spending the summer in Vermont, and there was a chorus of forest sounds lulling me to sleep—and then, suddenly, they stopped!"

Joe leaned forward, more interested in Hodding Wheatley's story than he had thought he'd be.

"The silence brought me completely back to my senses," Wheatley said softly. "I turned to the digital clock on my bedside, but it was dark, as though the power had failed. When I reached up and switched on the lamp, nothing happened."

The reporter grinned. "Sounds like a power failure."

"Ah, but then the lamp began to glow, only with an eerie light, and the digits on the clock radio began blinking. Suddenly a blinding light appeared in my window."

Wheatley held up his hands in front of his face, and Joe could almost see the light he was describing.

"I stumbled from the bed and into the hall. The light was dimmer there. I made my way to the front door and, still in my pajamas, ventured out into the night."

Gloria Forbin's eyes widened. "What did you find?"

"Darkness," Wheatley replied. "Yet I knew something was out there. Something that didn't belong. I walked into the forest, and suddenly *they* appeared."

"They?" the reporter looked at Hodding Wheatley rather oddly.

"Yes," Wheatley said, not paying attention to her reaction. "I couldn't immediately see who they were, but I heard voices speaking softly, in a language I'd never heard."

Ms. Forbin nodded knowingly. "An alien language."

"Yes, an alien language," Wheatley repeated. "Then, in the darkness, I felt hands pressing against me. Not hands in the conventional sense, but whatever they were, they pushed and prodded me toward an immense object in a clearing. Then a dim light appeared, and I saw that I was surrounded by tiny beings no taller than four feet, with smooth bulging heads and large eyes that glowed. They reached out to me with tentaclelike limbs and stroked my skin, always talking to me in that strange language."

54

Gloria Forbin frowned. "So you have no idea what these creatures were saying?"

"Strangely enough, I *did* begin to understand them," Wheatley said in an awe-filled voice. "It was almost as if they gave me the power to. They spoke to me of distant worlds and a life different from our own. They talked of love and knowledge, of great journeys and wonderful adventures."

"Umm. Sounds exciting," Ms. Forbin said with a touch of sarcasm.

"It was," Wheatley acknowledged. "I learned more in that evening than in my entire lifetime."

"And then what happened?" the reporter prompted.

Hodding Wheatley turned his gaze back to her. "After an almost dreamlike period, I found myself alone in the forest. And they were gone."

"Did they return?" the reporter asked.

"Several times," Wheatley replied with a slow smile. "And I hope they return again."

Gloria Forbin turned to the camera. "Well, you heard it here, ladies and gentlemen. The distinguished author Hodding Wheatley talking about his own kidnapping by aliens. And so, Mr. Wheatley, does this mean that you believe Fred Hawkins was actually kidnapped by a UFO yesterday evening in Bayport?"

"I try never to jump to conclusions," he answered. "But I think that's a distinct possibility."

"Thank you, Mr. Wheatley," the reporter said. "In a moment we'll be interviewing still more of the people involved in the Bayport UFO kidnapping!"

"That's our cue to head out of here," Frank whispered to Joe. "But before we do, I want to ask Wheatley something."

When the lights flickered off and the reporter went to talk to her crew, the Hardys pushed through the crowd that was gathered around Mr. Wheatley.

"That was quite a story," Frank said, walking up to the author.

"Yes," the man replied. "Did you believe it?"

"I didn't believe it for a minute," Joe scoffed.

Wheatley smiled. "So you think I concocted it so I could write a best-selling book?"

"Er, no," Joe stammered. "But you have to admit it *is* kind of hard to believe."

Wheatley grinned from ear to ear. "It is. And if it hadn't happened to me, I'd probably be as skeptical as you."

"What do you think about Fred Hawkins's kidnapping?" Frank asked. "Do you really think a UFO beamed down and swept him up?"

Wheatley shrugged. "I don't know. You'll have to tell me your side of the story."

Just then the restaurant lit up with the television camera lights, and Frank realized they were being filmed.

"Uh, Mr. Wheatley, do you mind stepping outside so we can finish our conversation in private?" Frank asked.

"Surely," Wheatley said.

The Hardys quickly walked through the crowd before Gloria Forbin could corner them. Once outside they related to Wheatley the events of the night before. When they were finished, Wheatley rubbed his chin and thought for a moment.

"Well," he said at last, "it does have some characteristics in common with a lot of well-known kidnappings. The high-pitched noise. The flashing lights. The way the UFO suddenly changed directions. Of course, anybody who's ever seen movies such as *The Great UFO Invasion* would already know about those things."

"I'm afraid I've never seen that movie," Frank said.

"So you think somebody faked the whole kidnapping?" Joe prompted.

The author held up his hands. "No, I didn't say that. It's possible that this is the real thing."

Frank and Joe looked at each other with raised brows.

Finally Frank shook his head and said,

"Thanks, Mr. Wheatley. Can we ask you some more questions in the future?"

"Which future are you talking about?" the man asked in an eerie voice.

When Joe's eyes widened in surprise, Wheatley clapped him on the back. "Just kidding," the writer said with a chuckle. "Now it's my turn for a question. Why are you two so interested in Fred Hawkins's kidnapping?"

"We're helping Mrs. Hawkins," Frank told him. "She asked us to help her find her husband."

Joe nudged his brother with his elbow. "Which is exactly what we'd better start doing!"

At six o'clock that evening the Bayport UFO story appeared on WBPT. The Hardys gathered around the television with their girlfriends. Callie and Iola applauded every time somebody they knew appeared on the screen.

Chet had his moment of glory, although the reporter referred to him as "Chet Norton." The Hardys appeared briefly, too. They were shown talking with Hodding Wheatley after his interview, and the reporter referred to Frank as Joe and to Joe as Frank.

"Why didn't she talk to you guys?" Iola asked, her eyes glued to the TV screen.

"We didn't want to steal the show away from Chet," Joe explained. He was sitting next to Iola, his arm draped around her shoulder.

Frank laughed. "He means we ducked out so the reporter couldn't get to us."

"And because you're not nearly as famous as 'Chet Norton,'" Callie teased.

As soon as the news was over, Iola jumped up. "I have a great idea," she said. "Let's go grab something to eat, then come back and watch the ten o'clock news. It's not often that I get to see my brother, my boyfriend, and *his* brother on TV!"

Joe rolled his eyes at the idea of watching the late news, but Iola was so excited that he couldn't say no. He stood up and turned to Frank and Callie. "Okay, guys, lets go. I'll eat anything— except another burger."

The loud jangle of the phone woke Joe up. He squinted at his digital clock. Seven o'clock in the morning! Joe answered with a sleepy mumble, expecting it to be a wrong number.

"Where's Fred Hawkins?" the voice on the other end demanded. It was a man's voice that Joe didn't recognize.

"Huh?" Joe replied, his brain still not fully alert.

"You know who I'm talking about," the voice

said. "Fred Hawkins from the Happy Burger restaurant. I heard you guys were tracking him down, and I want to know where he is."

Joe sat up. "Who is this?"

"Never mind," the voice said. "But I've got some words of advice for you punks. You better find Fred Hawkins before I do, or he's in big trouble!"

7 A Message from Beyond

"What kind of trouble?" Joe demanded. "And who is this?"

A clicking noise followed by a dial tone told Joe that the caller had hung up. Joe slipped on some shorts and rushed to Frank's bedroom.

"Wake up, lazybones." He shook Frank's shoulder. "We were just contacted by aliens from outer space."

Frank jerked upright. "What?"

"Just kidding," Joe said, laughing at Frank's reaction. "But we did get a call from someone very interested in finding Fred Hawkins."

"So the plot thickens," Frank said, swinging his legs to the side of the bed and running both hands through his hair. "Did the caller give you any idea why he wanted Mr. Hawkins?"

Joe nodded. "Yeah. It sounded as if he wanted to mess Fred's face up, if you catch my drift."

"Hmmm." Frank thought a moment as he pulled his jeans from the back of a chair. "Sounds suspiciously like our friendly loan shark."

"That's my guess."

"Well, maybe we ought to pay Mr. William Harbison a visit."

Half an hour later, while Aunt Gertrude served them bacon and pancakes, the two brothers discussed the case.

"You know," Joe said, waving his fork at Frank, "we've completely overlooked Clarissa Hawkins as a suspect."

"Fred's wife?" Frank looked doubtful.

Joe shrugged. "Why not? Maybe she's got a big insurance policy on him."

Frank burst out laughing. "I doubt an insurance company would pay up if they thought Clarissa's husband had been beamed up. No, if she wanted to get rid of him, she probably would've poisoned him or something."

"Then what do you think of those UFO Brigaders?" Joe asked. "Maybe they're so desperate for a sighting, they planned one themselves, and old Fred just happened to get in the way."

Frank stopped chewing, took a sip of juice,

then swallowed. "You may be right about the Brigaders. I'm just not sure what their motive would be. Any group that takes UFOs that seriously has to have some crackpots, though."

"Like Carl Thurmon," Joe said.

"Right," Frank said. He finished off the last bite of his pancakes, then said, "Let's call Mrs. Hawkins. We need to ask her about those loans and find out if the police have discovered anything new." He stood up and carried his empty plate to the sink.

"I'll also ask her about our mysterious caller," Joe said. "I wouldn't be surprised if it was somebody she knew."

Joe put his breakfast plate in the sink, too, and headed for the phone in his father's den. He looked up the Hawkinses' number in the phone book, then hesitated briefly before dialing. It was still early; he hoped he wouldn't wake Mrs. Hawkins up.

Clarissa Hawkins answered after the third ring. Her voice was sleepy but alert, as though she had been waiting for a phone call about bad news.

"Hello?" she said with some urgency. "Who is this?" she asked without waiting for Joe to identify himself.

"This is Joe Hardy. We just got a call from someone who knows your husband and apparently doesn't like him." Then he told her about the loan agreements with William Harbison. "The caller had a hoarse voice," he added. "Does it sound like anyone you know?"

Clarissa Hawkins sucked in her breath. "That sounds like the same person who kept calling Fred on the phone. Oh, I didn't realize Fred owed so much money. No wonder he was worried!"

Joe gave Frank the thumbs-up sign. "Is there anything else you can tell us that might help us find your husband? Have the police discovered anything new?"

There was a long pause on the other end of the line. "Uh, no," Clarissa Hawkins finally said. "But I'll let you know if anything comes up."

After saying goodbye, Joe slowly hung up the phone.

"That look on your face tells me something's not quite right," Frank said. "Was it something Mrs. Hawkins said?"

Joe rubbed his chin. "More like something she *didn't* say."

"You think she might be holding out on us?"

"It's hard to tell." Joe shrugged. "Maybe she was just searching her mind for some clue that might help us." Joe then told Frank that Mrs. Hawkins had said that a hoarse-voiced man had repeatedly called her husband about money he owed.

"Well, right now let's follow the clues we have," Frank said. "If Harbison has been calling

Fred Hawkins and threatening him about coming up with the money, he may just be part of this mystery."

Frank picked up the yellow pages and flipped through it to the section titled Loans. Mostly the listing consisted of banks and pawnshops. But there was a listing for something called the Harbison Group. "I found his office!" Frank exclaimed.

"He probably loaned Fred a large amount of money to start the Happy Burger, then socked him with huge amounts of interest," Frank said. "Then when business was slow and Fred couldn't pay up, Harbison started to threaten him."

Joe frowned. "Or maybe Harbison really did kill Fred."

"Then why would he call us?" Frank asked.

"To throw us off the trail, of course." Joe punched his brother on the shoulder. "Don't you ever watch detective shows?"

Frank rolled his eyes. "So that's where you learned how to be a detective," he joked, but then his expression turned serious. "Now I think it's time to pay our friendly loan shark a visit."

William Harbison's office was in a narrow building in a low-rent section of downtown Bayport. The office was located on the fourth floor of the run-down brownstone.

"Didn't you say the company was called the

Harbison *Group?*" Joe asked, looking up at the building. "I'll bet anything Harbison is a one-man group."

"Yeah," Frank agreed. "From the looks of the building, it's a pretty sleazy operation."

They entered the building and walked down a narrow, grimy hallway. There was no elevator, so the Hardys climbed the stairs to the fourth floor, where Harbison's office was located.

At the end of a dingy corridor Frank pointed to a sign that read "We Loan, You Gain."

"That should say 'We Loan, You Pay . . . and Pay and Pay,'" Joe whispered.

Frank chuckled and then knocked loudly on the door. Finally he heard a rattling sound as someone unlocked the door. Next it opened a crack. "Yeah, who is it?"

Joe turned to Frank and nodded. It was the same voice he had heard on the telephone.

"We'd like to borrow some money," Frank said. "We want to open a Mexican restaurant. Bayport needs tacos!"

The door opened wider, and a man with a skinny, ratlike face peered out. William Harbison had beady eyes, a scruffy mustache, and greased-back hair. "Yeah?" he said. "Tell me more."

Suddenly Joe stepped past Frank and kicked the door wide open. Startled, Harbison stumbled backward. "We'll tell you all about it as soon as you tell us about Fred Hawkins," Joe growled.

Frank rolled his eyes at Joe's imitation of a bad guy.

"Who?" Harbison replied. "I don't know any Fred Hawkins!" Reaching up to his collar, he nervously started to straighten his tie, then realized that he wasn't wearing one.

"Don't play dumb." Joe glared down at the little man. "Not only did you threaten Fred, you called me this morning and woke me up!"

William Harbison narrowed his eyes. "You two kids are the Hardy brothers?"

"That's us," Frank finally said, walking around the office. It was as sleazy-looking inside as it was outside.

Without turning his back on them, Harbison scuttled behind the metal desk and sat in a swivel chair. "Okay. So you guys are the big detectives I've heard of," he said, trying to make his voice sound menacing. "What do you want from me?"

"We want to know why you were threatening Fred Hawkins," Joe replied. Picking up Harbison's pen, he sat down on top of the desk and aimed the pen in the man's face. "And whether you had anything to do with his kidnapping."

Harbison shrugged. "How could I have had anything to do with his kidnapping? Everybody in town knows that a flying saucer took off with him. Weren't you guys there when it happened?"

"Yeah, we were," Frank said. "But we're not sure we believe in flying saucers."

67

"I'm sure I *don't* believe in flying saucers," Joe said emphatically. "My theory is some sleazy loan shark put pressure on him, and when Hawkins didn't cough up the money . . ." Joe made a slicing gesture across his throat.

Harbison jerked his head back. "Are you guys nuts? That isn't my line of work."

"Then what is it?" Frank asked. "Loaning people money at outrageous rates?"

Harbison looked insulted. "Hey, give me a break! I make my living loaning people money, so I have to make a decent amount in return."

"And Fred Hawkins was desperate enough to borrow from a creep like you?" Joe asked.

"He was pretty desperate, yeah," Harbison said. "After looking at his credit report, it was easy to see he'd failed at everything else he'd ever done. Naturally, I wanted him to pay somewhat higher interest than the local bank would ask."

"And now the guy owes you twenty thousand dollars," Frank said.

Harbison looked startled. "How'd you know that?"

Frank shrugged but said nothing.

"The guy made a few payments on the loan, then stopped about five months ago," Harbison explained. "I run a business, not a charity, which means I need that money back."

Resting his hands on the desk, Frank leaned closer to Harbison. "Any way you can?"

"Yeah." Joe glared at Harbison. "Like maybe you kidnapped him to get ransom money out of his wife."

Harbison sat up straight, an angry expression on his face. "Hey, show me a little respect, will you? I'll do a lot of things to make a client pay up, but kidnapping isn't one of them."

"Then why did you call us and threaten him?" Frank asked.

Harbison waved his hands nervously in the air. "I wanted to show the guy I meant business. I thought if you knew where he was, you could tell him so." Glancing back and forth at the Hardys, he said, "Hey, if the guy is hurt or dead, I'll never get the money out of him."

Joe stood up. "But you may be able to get the money out of his wife—get her to sell the house or something. We're on to you, Harbison." Frank noted the steely gaze his brother sent to the man.

"I don't go after women and children," Harbison protested.

"Okay, Harbison. We'll believe you for now," Frank said, straightening. "But we're going to keep an eye on you."

· "Fine," Harbison said. "Have it your way. But I didn't kidnap Fred Hawkins. And when I tell you that something is true, you can put money on it."

When Frank closed the door to Harbison's office, he had to clap a hand over his mouth to keep from laughing at his brother's tough guy act. "That was the worst imitation of a thug I've ever seen," he told Joe.

"Hey, it worked on that rat. We had him shaking in his boots."

Frank shook his head. "I doubt it. He just wanted us to think we had him scared."

"So Harbison seems to be hiding something," Joe guessed as they went down the stairs.

"Right," Frank agreed. "And it firms up another suspect, too."

"Fred himself," Joe said. "It's possible he staged his own kidnapping to get away from Harbison."

"Uh-huh," Frank said. "Or to get money to pay Harbison off."

"Come again?" Joe looked confused.

"Publicity for his restaurant," Frank said. "They're making money hand over fist in that place this week."

"Yeah, but that won't last," Joe said. "This UFO-mania will probably die down in a few days."

"Maybe," Frank said. "But publicity is publicity. Once people discover Chet's famous burgers, they'll keep coming back."

"Okay, I'll buy that," Joe said as they walked out of the building to their van. "But how could

70

Fred afford to stage a UFO kidnapping? That would have been quite a project, especially for a guy who's strapped for cash."

Frank sighed. "That's the problem." He got into the passenger side of the van.

Joe climbed into the driver's seat and started up the engine. "Where to now?"

"Let's stop by the library for a minute," Frank said. "I want to do some research on the UFO Brigade. Whoever engineered that UFO thing must've known a lot about it."

"You mean someone in the Brigade?"

Frank nodded. "Or Hodding Wheatley. He knows more than anyone. Maybe he decided a little more publicity would help the sale of his book."

At the library the Hardys looked up the UFO Brigade in a list of national organizations. They found a short paragraph describing it.

"They seem to be legit," Joe said. "But it says right here that they're not regarded as true UFOlogists. This book implies that they're more of a fringe group, but basically harmless."

"That's good to know," Frank said. "Except whoever wrote that information didn't know our friend Mr. Thurmon."

"That's for sure," Joe said, then sighed. "So where does that leave us now?"

"Still investigating," Frank replied.

After the Hardys left the library, they headed

straight for the Happy Burger. The crowd in the lot was so big that they had to drive up and down several aisles before they found a space.

By the time they parked, there was a long line of patrons waiting to get into the Happy Burger. In front of the restaurant was a hand-lettered sign announcing a special on Flying Saucer Burgers and Alien French Fries, with a side order of UFO Slaw. Next to the sign was a hand-drawn picture of the familiar smiling hamburger flying away on top of a saucer-shaped spaceship.

"Looks like Chet's artwork," Frank commented.

"Now I know why he never did well in art class," Joe added.

Frank noticed that there was some kind of show going on in the middle of the parking lot. A number of vans, bearing the name Sandra Rodriguez and Company, were parked nearby, and a large platform had been set up. In the middle of the stage a woman in her late thirties was talking into a microphone, interviewing someone perched on a chair. The woman doing the interview, who was dark-skinned and quite attractive, wore a tailored suit and appeared right at home in front of the three cameras that were aimed at her.

"Hi, Frank!" Callie Shaw shouted excitedly as the boys shoved their way into the crowd. "Over here!"

Frank and Joe pushed their way to where Callie and Iola were standing.

"What's going on?" Frank asked when he reached Callie's side.

"It's the Sandra Rodriguez show," Callie said excitedly. "It's going on the air live, right here from Bayport."

"Sandra Rodriguez?" Joe asked. "That talk show host on the *Mysteries Today* show?"

Iola nodded excitedly. "That's the one. Sandra Rodriguez is the one who investigates strange phenomena. Yesterday she interviewed several women who claimed to have alien husbands. And today she's broadcasting her show live from Bayport."

"If she's doing a special show about the kidnapping of Fred Hawkins, why aren't we included?" Joe said in a mock-angry tone. "We were the ones who saw Fred disappear."

Callie's face brightened. "Why don't you two go up onstage and ask to be interviewed? Then you'll really be celebrities."

"I was just kidding," Joe said quickly.

"We've done pretty well *avoiding* interviews," Frank added. "Maybe the next time a UFO lands in Bayport, though, we'll talk to Sandra Rodriguez about it."

"Suit yourself," Iola said in a disappointed voice.

Standing on tiptoe, Frank looked over the

73

heads of the crowd to get a closer look at the stage. Sandra Rodriguez was still in the middle of the interview. Next to her on the stage, just out of the range of the camera, was a handsome, muscular man in blue jeans and a casual shirt, who looked to be in his mid-forties.

"Who's that guy?" Frank asked Callie. "Is he part of Sandra Rodriguez's show, too?"

"That's Matt Everson, Rodriguez's boyfriend," Callie said impatiently. "He's also the producer of the show and her personal manager."

Joe hit the side of his head with his palm. "How stupid of us not to recognize him," he joked.

"So what's the big deal about Mr. Matt Hunk Everson?" Frank asked.

"He's a national hero," Callie said. "He received the Congressional Medal of Honor for service in Vietnam, where he was a helicopter pilot for a group of medics. Not to mention how cute he is."

Callie and Iola made swooning motions and leaned back against their boyfriends. Frank and Joe looked at each other in disgust.

"Sorry we asked," Frank said. "Are you guys ready for lunch? The line for the Happy Burger looks as though it's getting longer."

"And miss this?" Callie said. "Not a chance. We'll join you later."

Frank and Joe waved goodbye, then made their

74

way through the crowd. The end of the line stopped by the window of an electronics store.

"Look!" Joe exclaimed in mock excitement, pointing to the window. "We can still watch the show."

Frank looked where his brother was pointing. Sure enough, the woman they saw on the make-shift stage was also visible on several of the television screens in the window.

Suddenly the picture changed, and Sandra Rodriguez was replaced by a message in large letters that flashed across the screen of all the televisions.

"Whoops!" Joe chuckled. "They're having problems. Must have lost their signal to the network."

Frank frowned as he stared at the screen. "No. It's something else," he said. "Look!"

PLEASE LISTEN TO US. WE CANNOT TELL YOU WHO WE ARE, BECAUSE YOU WOULD NOT UNDERSTAND. WE HAVE TAKEN THE INDIVIDU-AL WHOM YOU CALL FRED HAWKINS AS PART OF OUR STUDY OF YOUR PLANET. WE NOW WISH TO RETURN HIM TO YOU. YOU WILL FIND HIM IN A SHORT TIME, IN THE PLACE THAT YOU CALL BAYPORT MEADOWS.

8 Waiting for Fred

Frank stared at the message in astonishment. "Let's go!" he exclaimed. "Bayport Meadows is only two miles from here."

Joe put a restraining hand on his brother's arm. "Wait a minute," he said. "Let's see what happens. This might be just another hoax."

After remaining on the screen for several minutes, the message faded away, and Joe saw Sandra Rodriguez reappear.

"This is amazing!" the talk show host exclaimed, staring at a small TV monitor that sat next to her on the platform. "I've never seen anything like this! We appear to have received a communication from whoever—or whatever—kidnapped Fred Hawkins!"

"And I've never seen anything like it, either," Joe said. "Why would the aliens put a message on *Mysteries Today?*"

"Maybe they bought advertising time, like everybody else," Frank cracked. "Look, we can go up to the production crew and find out what happened, or we can be the first to get to Bayport Meadows."

"Bayport Meadows," Joe said quickly as he took off toward the van. But by the time they were on the road, the traffic was already so heavy with people trying to get from the shopping center to Bayport Meadows that cars weren't moving. In frustration Joe pulled the van onto the side of the road.

"I say we park the van and run the two miles," he suggested.

Frank agreed. It took them almost twenty minutes to jog to Bayport Meadows, a large field behind a housing development. The field was surrounded on three sides by woods.

Already a crowd had formed there. In fact, in the time that it had taken Frank and his brother to get there, half of Bayport seemed to have put in an appearance. Groups of people stood around looking at the grass, the trees, and one another. Sandra Rodriguez's crew had managed to get there in record time. They were quickly setting up the equipment for a remote broadcast from the meadow. Also, one UFO Brigade van was parked on the edge of the field, and several Brigaders were wandering among the crowd, glancing around curiously.

"How'd Rodriguez's crew get here so fast?" Joe asked his brother.

Frank shook his head. "Makes you kind of wonder if they knew in advance that the aliens were going to choose Bayport Meadows. I wonder where Rodriguez is, though. Just the crew seems to be here."

Joe shrugged, and craning his neck, he looked over the crowd. "And where's Fred? I thought those aliens said he'd be here in a 'short time.'"

"Maybe they just haven't dropped him off yet," Frank suggested. "Besides, how do we know what a bunch of aliens mean by 'a short time'? They might think five weeks is a short time. After all, the aliens are dealing with light-years."

Joe chuckled. "I think you're starting to sound like Hodding Wheatley. Which reminds me, where *is* the best-selling author? I would've thought he'd be in the middle of all this."

"There he is." Frank pointed across the field. Hodding Wheatley was standing on the edge of the crowd, surveying the scene. Joe motioned for Frank to follow as he headed over to him.

"How are you doing, Mr. Wheatley?" Joe asked. "And what do you think of the latest news about Fred Hawkins being dropped off in this field by the aliens?"

Wheatley shrugged, a look of faint amusement on his face. "I'm not sure what to make of it. This case certainly is curious. For instance, aliens almost never engage in public communications, such as the one we just saw on television. But I suppose there's a first time for everything."

Several of the UFO Brigaders walked past. Carl Thurmon was in the middle of the group. He glared at Joe but never broke stride. Then he picked up a small walkie-talkie and spoke into it, but Joe was too far away to hear what he was saying.

When Thurmon finished speaking on the walkie-talkie, he turned and said something to his companions. Joe watched intently as they all did an about-face and headed for the van they'd parked on the edge of the field.

"What about these UFO Brigade guys?" Frank gestured toward the departing group.

"I'm acquainted with the Brigade," Wheatley replied. "I've even lectured at some of their conventions. They have a very strong commitment to exploring UFO phenomena. Perhaps too strong a commitment."

"That's what I thought," Joe said.

Wheatley looked over his shoulder to see if anyone was listening, then leaned closer to the Hardys. "They genuinely believe that the United States government is actively involved in covering up contact with aliens."

"And you don't?" Frank asked in a low voice.

"Not exactly," Wheatley said. "Oh, there's no question that our government studies UFOs, just as it studies every other object flying in the vicinity of Earth. They'd be insane not to. They need to track everything they detect in orbital space, so that our satellites and space shuttles don't get pelted with debris. And of course they also need to make sure that some country doesn't start World War Three with a sneak attack."

"And have they actually observed UFOs?" Joe asked in a voice filled with doubt.

Wheatley nodded. "But remember, the term *UFO* is simply an abbreviation for *unidentified flying object.* Not all UFOs are spaceships from other planets. An airplane or a weather balloon can be a UFO, as long as nobody's identified it yet. Most UFOs turn out to be things exactly like that."

"Most?" Frank repeated.

"Yes," Wheatley said. "Most. But every now and then a UFO pops up that can't be identified so easily. A few that did some pretty unusual things while they were here never *have* been identified."

Frank's eyes widened. "Like what?"

"Like flying rings around the fastest jet planes ever built," Wheatley explained in his mesmerizing voice. "Like coming to a halt in midair so suddenly that anyone inside should have been crushed. Like causing machines on the ground below to go berserk."

"That's creepy." Joe shook his head. "I mean, not that I believe in any of this stuff. Unless . . ." He eyed Wheatley for a moment. "Has the government ever really proved that a UFO was actually a spaceship?"

Wheatley sighed. "I'm afraid the answer is no. But they've certainly proved that the sightings themselves were real, not figments of somebody's imagination."

"So is it true that the government is covering all this up?" Frank asked.

"Well, they're not exactly eager to talk about it," Wheatley said. "A lot of the information concerning the government's search for UFOs is classified. In some cases, this is because the information was gathered through the use of tools such as observation satellites that are themselves top secret. In other cases I honestly think the government feels a little silly about being in the UFO-hunting business and would rather pretend that it isn't involved. UFO hunting is supposed to be for crazy writers who do books about flying saucers," he said with a chuckle.

"How far do you think the Brigaders would go to keep the government from covering up a UFO incident like this one?" Frank asked.

Wheatley frowned. "That's hard to say. I don't think the Brigaders are dangerous. But they *are* rather zealous in their quest for contact with extraterrestrials."

"Zealous enough to stage a UFO incident themselves?" Frank pressed.

"I don't think so. What would they gain by that?"

"Do you know that guy Carl Thurmon?" Joe broke in. "It seems to me he'd do anything if he thought someone was in his way."

Wheatley made a gesture of dismissal. "Thurmon's all bark and no bite."

Joe snorted. "Not from what I saw the other day. What's wrong with him, anyway?"

"When he served in the Vietnam War, he stepped on a land mine and nearly died. For hours he was in a deep coma, and when he awoke he was convinced that he had been visited by an alien who saved his life. He said the alien made him promise to spread the message about other beings in return for the favor. I'm afraid the incident pushed him over the edge. Lately, he suspects everyone of standing in the way of the alien message."

"Talking about Brigaders," Frank suddenly said, "their van just pulled away. Do you think they know something we don't?"

Wheatley looked in the direction of the departing van. "Maybe they've decided that Mr. Hawkins isn't going to show up."

"Maybe we should follow them," Joe said.

Just then there was a soft but familiar noise from the skies—the beating of helicopter blades. Joe looked up to see a medium-size chopper appear from behind a bank of trees and land in the far corner of the field. As soon as it touched down, the hatch opened, and out stepped Sandra Rodriguez. A moment later her helicopter pilot boyfriend climbed out the other side. As if on cue, the television crew began moving their equipment in her direction.

"Looks as if the Sandra Rodriguez show is back on the air," Joe said. "Maybe Fred will beam back to earth now that he knows he'll be on TV."

"Let's go hear what the entertainment queen has to say," Frank suggested. He pushed his way through the crowd, his brother right behind him, until they were close enough to hear Sandra Rodriguez speaking into her microphone. Apparently the show was back on the air, because there was a glowing red light on one of the cameras pointed at her.

"We're broadcasting live again, this time from a large field on the outskirts of the tiny town of Bayport," she was saying, "reporting on what may turn out to be the hottest story of the twentieth century."

Putting his hand in front of his mouth, Joe leaned toward Frank. "Don't you think she's exaggerating just a little?" he whispered.

Frank chuckled. "I'd say she's got a lot of nerve calling Bayport a tiny town."

"While my pilot and I were circling the field in our helicopter," Rodriguez went on, "we noticed something interesting in one corner." She gestured toward her left. Joe could see an empty section of the field in front of the woods. "An almost perfect circle of crushed grass, as though a heavy object had recently been sitting on the ground there. Could this be the landing site of the flying saucer?"

Frank and Joe exchanged surprised glances. Then Joe spun around and raced toward the section of field where Sandra had pointed. This time he wasn't going to let the crowd beat him to it.

When Joe reached the area, he discovered that the grass *was* crushed in a circular pattern about twenty feet across, roughly the same size as the UFO they had seen land near the Happy Burger. Then he noticed something else. In the middle of the field was a scrap of white paper.

Quickly Joe ran over and picked it up, using a bandanna so that he wouldn't smudge any fingerprints that might be on it. It was a small, rectangular sheet that had been ripped from a memo pad. On the top of it were the words Happy Burger.

Joe frowned. Anyone could have thrown it on the ground, he thought. But then he turned it over, and his mouth dropped open. On the back of the sheet, written in shaky letters, was the word *Help.*

9 The Grounded UFO

"What did you find?" Frank asked as he approached Joe.

Joe carefully handed him the bandanna and the paper. "I think Fred Hawkins was trying to communicate with us."

Frank frowned as he turned over the paper and studied both sides. "We don't know he wrote it."

"What about the fact that it's on Happy Burger notepaper?" Joe pointed out.

"True. But anyone could've swiped a piece of memo paper from the restaurant."

"Excuse me!" called Sandra Rodriguez, bounding toward them from across the field. "Did you boys discover some exciting clue that a UFO landed here?"

Frank quickly wrapped the paper in the bandanna and stuck it in his pocket. The talk show host must have noticed because she thrust the microphone in his face and inquired in a frosty voice, "I hope you're not withholding important evidence?"

Frank shook his head. "No. I'm taking it right to the police." He gestured toward two officers in the distance directing traffic. "The detective on this case will want to see it."

Ms. Rodriguez signaled to the crew to stop the cameras. "The—the police?" she stammered. After handing the microphone to an assistant, she shot Frank a haughty look. "The police think this whole UFO thing is a fraud. *I'm* the one who will use the information to discover the truth."

Frank heard Joe chuckle.

"The police may think the UFO is a fraud, but I'm sure they take Fred's disappearance very seriously," Frank said. "Now, if you'll excuse me."

Sandra's face turned red. Then she turned and motioned toward the crew. "Follow those boys to the police officers and find out what they've got. Quick!"

Frank winked at Joe as the two took off across the field, Sandra and her crew tagging along behind them. The Hardys handed over the paper to an officer and explained where they'd found it.

Sandra Rodriguez made certain she heard every word the Hardys said.

Then, microphone in hand again, she turned back to the camera. "You heard it right here, ladies and gentlemen!" she exclaimed in a theatrical voice. "The latest development in the Bayport UFO kidnapping case. A note has been found in the middle of what appears to be a UFO landing site. And the terse message written on it was 'Help.' Was this Fred Hawkins's desperate cry to be rescued from his alien abductors?"

"Or was it a note from a viewer sick of watching Sandra Rodriguez's stupid show?" Joe whispered in Frank's ear.

Frank chuckled. "You've got that right. Now that I think about it, it seems pretty hokey to think a UFO would land long enough in Bayport Meadows to let Fred Hawkins drop his message, then take off into outer space again."

"Agreed," Joe said, pulling his brother back into the crowd. "Come on, let's check out the UFO landing site before a hundred gawkers trample it flat."

When they left, Frank could still hear Sandra Rodriguez droning on about poor, desperate Fred Hawkins out in space trying to escape his evil abductors.

Joe stopped so suddenly that Frank almost ran into him. "We're too late."

Frank looked over his brother's shoulder. The

circle where the UFO had supposedly landed was practically picked clean of vegetation. A mob was milling around, so even the indentation was no longer visible. Frank watched as a young boy held up a scraggly weed to show his friend. "Who knows," the kid cried, "an alien might've stepped on this plant!"

"Am I dreaming all this?" Joe asked in a bewildered voice. "Or maybe we're extras in a science fiction movie and don't realize it."

Frank sighed and shook his head. "No. This is real. We're just not used to having a close encounter with serious UFOlogists."

Joe raised his brows. "Serious? These folks are wacky if you ask me."

"Well, so much for clues," Frank said. "What do you make of Sandra Rodriguez?"

Joe snorted. "She's not the best TV interviewer I've ever seen."

"That wasn't what I meant," Frank said. "Don't you think it's more than a coincidence that she showed up so quickly in the middle of all this? And that she's the one who 'discovered' the landing spot?"

"Definitely. And I think she's the type to do anything to boost her ratings," Joe added.

As the Hardys started to hike back to the van, Frank said, "So when nothing exciting was happening, she and that Matt Everson guy decided to create a little drama."

"They could have made that indentation by rolling something heavy over the area," Joe said. "And any one of their crew could have snitched a memo pad from the Happy Burger. Chet and Louise are so busy they'd never have noticed."

"It'll be interesting to find out from the police if there are any fingerprints on that note," Frank added.

Joe looked at his brother. "Do aliens have fingerprints?"

Frank laughed. "We'll soon find out."

Just then Frank heard the sound of helicopter blades beating the air. When he glanced behind him, he could still see Sandra Rodriguez interviewing people in the crowd. Matt Everson was at the controls of the helicopter.

"I wonder where *he's* headed," Joe said. "You were saying that we ought to keep an eye on him."

"Yeah," Frank said. "And if we can get back to the van in time, it shouldn't be too hard to tail a helicopter."

The two Hardys took off at a fast sprint. By the time they reached the van, Frank was sweating. He unlocked the door and jumped into the driver's seat.

"He just took off," Joe said, shading his face with his hand and looking in the direction of Bayport Meadows. "And we're in luck. He's headed this way."

Joe jumped into the passenger side, slamming the door just as Frank pulled onto the road. Ducking down, Frank looked out the windshield and said, "Looks as if he's heading north into the country."

Joe shot Frank a puzzled look. "There aren't any airports in that direction."

"Then let's just find out where our hero is going," Frank said as he stepped on the gas.

Within minutes they were driving down a one-lane road between several large farms. The helicopter was just in sight, flying low over the green fields.

"Hey, he's starting to go down," Joe said.

Frank slowed the car and watched as the helicopter circled, then began its descent.

"Everson seems to be landing in a farmyard," Joe said. He'd rolled down the window and hung halfway out, trying to get a better look. "I can see a big red barn, and the chopper's just disappeared behind it." Joe ducked back into the van.

Up ahead Frank could see a dirt tractor path leading into a field of corn. Turning right, he steered the van down the bumpy lane.

"Let's wait here and see if Everson leaves," he told his brother. "Seems kind of peculiar that he'd keep his helicopter out in the middle of nowhere."

"You mean like he's got something to hide," Joe commented.

91

Frank nodded. "Yeah. And I'd like to take a look inside that barn."

About ten minutes later a blue sports car zoomed past them. "It's Everson," Frank said, starting up the van again. When he turned up the dirt drive to the farm, he could see that the house was boarded up.

Frank parked the van in Everson's fresh tire tracks. Then the two brothers climbed out and walked around to the back of the barn. Everson's helicopter was sitting in the middle of a grassy field.

Frank turned back to study the barn while Joe checked out the helicopter. Facing Frank were two doors large enough for hay wagons to pass through. The doors were locked tight. Beside them was a smaller door. Frank rattled the handle.

"It's locked, too," he called to Joe. "Must be something pretty valuable in there."

Joe jogged over to him. "Helicopter looks normal. Let's take a look in the barn," he said, pointing to a window about ten feet off the ground. "There's no glass in it. If you give me a boost, I should be able to climb through."

Frank followed his brother to the side of the barn. "No. You give *me* a boost. On our last case you got to do the exciting stuff while I was lookout."

"Oh, all right." Crouching down, Joe laced his

fingers together. Frank put one foot in his brother's palms. With a grunt Joe lifted him toward the window.

Frank could barely reach the sill. Joe boosted him higher.

"Whew!" Joe gasped from below. "Would you hurry up?"

Frank grabbed on to the wooden sill and pulled himself up until he could get one leg across it. Straddling the windowsill, he lowered his head and stuck it inside the barn. It took a minute for his eyes to adjust to the darkness, but once they did, he could make out something large on the floor below. Pulling a tiny flashlight from his pocket, he aimed it into the dusty barn. The faint beam traveled across the floor, illuminating a familiar, dome-shaped object.

"Joe, I found it!" Frank called down to his brother. "I found the UFO that kidnapped Fred Hawkins!"

10 Inside a UFO

"All right!" Joe cried excitedly from outside. "Now we just need to find our bogus aliens so they can lead us to Fred. Then we'll have cracked this case wide open, big brother!"

"I'll jump down into the barn and let you in the door," Frank called.

Joe watched as Frank pulled his other leg through the window and then disappeared inside the barn. He jogged to the door just as Frank pulled it open.

As Joe stepped inside, a beam of sunlight illuminated the interior of the barn, playing across the surface of the UFO. It looked exactly as it had the night it had flown into the parking lot, except that the ring of lights was now dark. The exterior of the saucer was a shiny material that seemed to glow in the light. The domelike top rose up about fifteen feet from the hay-covered floor.

"So this is the famous Bayport UFO," Joe said. When he stopped speaking, he realized how quiet the barn was. There was no sign or sound of life. For a second Joe had to suppress a shiver.

Frank walked up to the side of the UFO and knocked on it gently with his knuckles. The sound echoed.

"It's hollow," Frank said.

Moving closer, Joe ran his hands over the surface. "Unless I miss my guess, this thing is made out of plastic—as in 'Made in the USA,' not on Mars."

"Still, you have to admit that it looks pretty realistic in the dark," Frank said, playing the beam of the flashlight across it. "And that's all it needed to do, since it kidnapped Fred at night. And look, the plastic is covered with silver glitter to give it a cosmic look when light hits it. That's why it seems to glow."

"I wonder if we can get inside." Joe walked slowly around the craft. He spotted a small hinged door just above ground level. He grabbed the metal handle.

"Are you ready for your first alien encounter?"

he asked Frank with a grin. "Who knows? Maybe we'll meet some of those little guys with big eyes that Hodding Wheatley talks about."

Frank chuckled. "Those guys wouldn't be caught dead in a crummy spaceship like this."

Joe pulled the door open and, ducking low, looked inside. He pulled his own flashlight out of his pants pocket and pointed it around the interior. The UFO was a hollow plastic shell. Around the curved sides were yards and yards of electrical wires.

Frank bent down next to Joe and said, "All those wires must supply power to the flashing lights on the outside of the craft."

In the interior were a pair of boxes, placed directly across from each other. Each had a large speaker attached to it.

"Noise generators," Joe said as he stepped through the doorway. "That must be how the ship made the whining sound when it landed."

Directly in the center of the interior, a series of ropes hung down from the ceiling, forming a kind of hanging web. Joe poked around at the ropes, then pulled up into the middle of the web.

"It's like a hammock seat," he declared. "I bet this is where Fred Hawkins sat while he took his little ride."

"Now the question is, was he forced inside, or did he climb in willingly?" Frank wondered.

Joe snorted. "This thing isn't big enough for two people. I bet he opened up the door, stepped inside, closed the door, and sat in that seat—which he easily could have done in ten seconds." Joe grabbed at a piece of rope dangling from the ceiling. When he pulled on it, there was a clicking noise from above. "And this was how he sent a signal to the pilot saying that he was ready for lift-off."

"Pilot?" Frank asked. "Where would the pilot sit? Besides, there's no engine in this thing."

"It's not hard to figure out where the pilot was," Joe said, climbing out of the web. He exited the saucer and aimed his flashlight up toward the top of the saucer's curved exterior. At the very peak of the dome was a metal hitch that resembled the tow hitch on the back of a truck. A jet-black metal cable was dangling from it. The cable, which was several hundred feet long, fell to the floor of the barn, where it lay in a pile.

"The other end of that cable must have been attached to Matt Everson's helicopter," Joe said. "With Everson several hundred feet up in the air, the noise generator would have drowned out the sound of his blades. Although now that I think about it, that night I *did* hear another sound over the noise of the UFO. That must have been the chopper."

"Everson must have been flying with his lights

out," Frank added. "We were so dazzled by all the flashing lights on this stupid saucer that we never noticed he was there."

Joe shook his head in amazement. "Boy, Everson and Hawkins sure must have spent a lot of time working out this charade," Joe said. "Everson dropped the saucer to the ground right in front of Fred, who opened the door and climbed inside. Then Everson took off again, making it look like the saucer was making a fancy U-turn in the air. Actually, it was just being dragged along behind a helicopter."

"How could it make a ninety-degree turn in midair, though?" Frank asked. "Even a helicopter can't do that."

Joe raised his hands in the air, one on top of the other. "Because it was being towed *underneath* the copter," he explained. "Think back to physics class. Remember when we learned about inertia? You know, the tendency of an object to move in the same direction unless acted on by an outside force."

Frank whistled. "I'm impressed, little brother. And all this time I thought you slept through that class."

Joe ignored Frank's joke. "The UFO kept going straight when the helicopter turned. Then, when the cable pulled taut, the UFO was suddenly yanked in another direction, making it look from the ground like a ninety-degree turn." With a sweeping motion of his lower hand, Joe demonstrated what he was talking about.

Just then the silence was broken by the sound of a door opening. Joe blinked as light flooded into the barn. He shaded his eyes, trying to see who it was. A dark figure stood silhouetted in the doorway. Joe nudged his brother.

"Don't look now, Frank," he whispered, "but I think we're going to experience a close encounter with a very angry helicopter pilot."

"What are you boys doing here?" Matt Everson demanded as he strode toward them. He had a pistol in his hand, which he was pointing directly at them. "You're trespassing on private property! I ought to call the police."

"Go ahead," Joe told him. "Last I heard, trespassing wasn't as serious an offense as kidnapping."

Everson stopped in his tracks. The barn was silent as the pilot glanced back and forth at the two Hardys. But with a steady hand, he kept the gun aimed at them. "What are you talking about?" he said with a sneer.

"You know what we're talking about," Frank replied. "This is the mystery ship that was used to kidnap Fred Hawkins the other night. Since you knew it was here, it's pretty obvious you were involved with the kidnapping."

"Who are you guys?" Everson demanded. "Wait. I bet you punks think you can blackmail me. Well, you're not getting anything except tied up and dumped in that saucer you're so curious about. Now move!" Waving the gun, Everson motioned them toward the door of the saucer.

Slowly Joe raised his hands in the air. "Uh, I think you've got us all wrong," he tried to explain.

"Shut up," Everson growled.

Frank and Joe began to back toward the door to the spaceship. Joe tilted his head, trying to catch Frank's eye. When Frank glanced his way, he gave his brother a faint nod.

"It's the cops!" Joe suddenly hollered, and at the same time the two Hardys dived for Everson's legs.

Grunting loudly, the pilot fell on his back. With a practiced movement, Joe snatched the gun from Everson's grasp.

Frank grabbed Everson's wrist and jerked the man into a sitting position. But instead of resisting, Everson began to shake his head and laugh.

"It's two against one," he said, looking up at them and rubbing the small of his back with his other hand. "Besides, I'm too old for this."

"Then what's with all the nasty threats?" Frank asked.

Everson shrugged. "When you see guys doing it all the time on TV, you figure it'll work. And I used to be tough when I was in the military."

Joe checked the cylinder of the small pistol. "It's not even loaded," he told Frank.

Everson looked up at the two Hardys. "So are you two here to demand silence money or something?"

"No." Joe stood up. "We're detectives, not blackmailers. We're trying to track down Fred Hawkins."

"And obviously you know something about this kidnapping," Frank added. He let go of Everson's wrist and jumped to his feet.

With a deep sigh Everson rubbed his fingers against his temples, then stood up. "It's not that simple," he said.

"You mean you were in it with a bunch of aliens?" Joe quipped.

"Look." Everson threw up his hands. "I had nothing to do with Fred Hawkins's being kidnapped because Fred Hawkins wasn't kidnapped. He *wanted* to disappear."

"That was one of our theories," Frank said.

"He was in some kind of money trouble," Everson continued. "When he told us the UFO idea, Sandra and I mulled it over for a while, then figured it might be good for ratings. Her show has dropped from number five to number twenty-five. It wouldn't have been long before the network canceled it."

"So she figured this UFO thing would boost her ratings?" Joe asked.

"Exactly," Everson said. "I told her she was crazy, but she wouldn't give up the idea. Sandra can be very persuasive when she wants to be. Eventually she talked me into it, though I never stopped having second thoughts."

"How did Hawkins get in touch with you?" Frank asked.

"Fred was in Vietnam," Everson said. "So was I. We didn't know each other during the war, but I went to an officers' reunion a few months ago, and Fred was there. He'd worked out this whole UFO scheme himself, but he needed someone to help him with it."

"So it *was* all Fred's idea." Frank grinned at Joe. "Well, little brother, as soon as we find out where Mr. Hawkins is, we can close this case, and I can go back to having a leisurely summer vacation."

The pilot's face reddened. "I wish it was that easy."

Frank and Joe looked at him with puzzled expressions.

Everson nervously cleared his throat, then said, "This time Fred Hawkins really *has* disappeared."

11 The Money Trail

"Fred Hawkins really *has* disappeared?" Frank repeated in disbelief.

Joe rolled his eyes. "You expect us to believe you?"

Matt shrugged. "We don't know what happened to him. He was staying in the boarded-up farmhouse." He nodded in the direction of the house. "We rented this property, and Fred was going to hide out until the aliens dropped him off at Bayport Meadows. At least, that was the plan."

"And what went wrong?" Frank asked.

"I don't know," Everson replied. "Early this morning, before it was even light, I drove Fred to the woods by the meadow. Last night we'd matted the grass down so it looked as if the UFO had landed. Fred was supposed to hide out after that, then make his way to the landing site by noon. Only when Sandra and her crew arrived at Bayport Meadows, there was no sign of him."

"Except for the note," Frank added. "No wonder she wanted it. You know, Everson"—Frank eyed the pilot—"you and Ms. Rodriguez could get into big trouble for this."

"I don't think so. Sandra and I checked out all the legal angles before we went through with it," Everson said. "It wasn't a real kidnapping, so we didn't break the law. Plus we signed an agreement with Fred, which stated that since he engineered the whole UFO hoax, we couldn't be held liable."

"And I bet for a big sum of money, you made sure he'd never mention your involvement," Joe added.

Everson smiled briefly. "That wasn't quite it. Obviously, he didn't have enough money to pull off the hoax—to rent the property and buy the supplies to build the flying saucer. We gave him the money—invested in the idea, so to speak. We figured the investment was worth it. Sandra's show would get a lot of publicity. And you have to remember that in television, any publicity is good publicity."

"How did you and Hawkins build this thing, anyway?" Frank asked, rapping on the curved side of the saucer.

"Easy. I knew several special effects experts in the industry who were happy to contribute their know-how. Fred bought the materials and did the actual building."

Joe put his hands on his hips and looked squarely at Everson. "You know we're going to have to tell the police about this."

The pilot frowned. "I was hoping you'd give us some time to find Fred first. Sandra and I can still make our scheme work. If you blow it now, all of us will look like fools."

"Uh, let me talk to my brother a minute," Frank said. He gestured for Joe to follow him around to the other side of the saucer. "So what do you think?"

Joe shook his head. "It's a hard one to call. I mean, Fred's kidnapping didn't really hurt anyone."

"Except maybe Clarissa Hawkins."

Joe shrugged. "Maybe not. Maybe that's why she was so hesitant on the phone. Maybe Fred had contacted her and let her know he was okay."

"Could be," Frank said. "So you think we should help Everson find him?"

"Why not?" Joe replied. "That's what we were hired to do—find Fred Hawkins—no matter what crazy thing he's cooked up now. Besides," he said, grinning, "this is just getting interesting."

"Okay, Everson," Frank said when they walked back to the front of the saucer. "We won't go to the police or the press—yet. But you'd better be telling the truth when you say you don't know where Hawkins is."

Matt Everson nodded, a relieved expression on his face. "And I'll let you know if we find out anything. I'm staying at the Bayport Inn with Sandra and the crew. Call if you hear anything."

Frank, Joe, and Everson walked out into the blinding sunlight.

"Why did you come back here, anyway?" Frank asked as Everson locked the barn door.

"I saw you guys parked off the road," he said. "Remember, I was in Vietnam. I've got eyes in the back of my head. I didn't know who you were, but a van in a cornfield is pretty suspicious."

Frank grinned. "That's kind of how we operate, too. We followed your helicopter on a hunch, and look what happened."

"Yeah. Nothing," Joe grumbled. "We're right back where we started—searching for Fred Hawkins."

Frank held up his index finger. "Yes, but at least this time we're looking for a human kidnapper, not an alien abductor. That should make things a little easier."

They said goodbye, and Joe and Frank walked back to their van.

"So what now?" Joe said minutes later as Frank drove away from the farm. "Who do we investigate now that the whole case has been turned on its ear?"

"I think we'd better grab some lunch, then see what our friend Harbison is up to," Frank suggested.

"I thought we scratched him as a suspect."

"That was before we knew Fred Hawkins had really disappeared," Frank said. "If Harbison is desperate to get that money from Hawkins, maybe he discovered where Hawkins was staying and followed him to Bayport Meadows. Then, after Everson left, maybe he confronted Hawkins."

"Only Hawkins would've convinced Harbison that he'd be getting the money as soon as the hoax was over," Joe said. "So there was no need for any strong-arm tactics."

Frank shot Joe a get-with-it look. "Unless Harbison is only a little spit of water in a big pond."

"Huh?" Joe was puzzled.

"Where does Harbison get *his* money? Twenty thousand dollars is a lot of cash."

"Ohhh." Joe's eyebrows shot up. "You mean Harbison borrowed the money from some shady guy, who wants it back *now*."

"Or maybe yesterday," Frank said as he turned into the drive-through lane of a fast-food restaurant. "What do you want to eat?"

"Anything except a burger."

After picking up their order of BLTs and iced teas, the Hardys drove to Harbison's office, parked across the street, and waited. Joe ate his sandwich, then put his head back on the seat. Even though they'd parked in the shade, it felt as if it were a hundred degrees inside the van.

Joe was dreaming about UFOs when someone shook his shoulder roughly.

"Joe! Wake up," Frank said urgently. "There's Harbison."

Blinking sleepily, Joe looked up. Harbison was walking swiftly to a green car parked in front of his office. He glanced right and left as if to make sure no one was watching, then climbed into his car and drove off.

Joe snapped awake. "Let's go, big brother."

They followed Harbison to the edge of town, keeping a safe distance between the van and his car. After a few more minutes Harbison turned into the front drive of a large mansion in one of the wealthier parts of Bayport.

Frank pulled the van off on the side of the road about fifty yards away, where shrubbery shielded it from view. The Hardys climbed out of the van and, stooping low, made their way to a thick hedge surrounding the property.

"I wonder who lives here," Joe said. Peering over the top of the hedge, he looked around. The three-story house was made of brick, with a wide expanse of manicured lawn. Joe could make out a pool and tennis court in the backyard.

"I don't know," Frank said. "But they've got to be rich."

"Rich enough to lend Harbison money?" Joe asked.

"That rich," Frank replied. "And my guess is, whoever lives here is some Bayport businessman who runs a legitimate operation in town. On the side he runs a loan business. After all, where else can your money make over fifteen percent interest?"

Joe snorted. "Not the bank, that's for sure. I think my savings account gets five percent, if that."

"Right. And I bet a sleazeball like Harbison is only the front man. The guy inside the mansion is probably calling all the shots."

"Well, if we're going to prove any of this, we'd better take a closer look," Joe said, starting to stand up.

Frank yanked him back down. "What were you going to do—stroll right up to the front door, ring the bell, and ask if we could borrow some money?"

Joe shrugged. "Worked with Harbison."

"That's 'cause he's just a lackey." Frank thought a minute, then snapped his fingers. "Hey, don't we have our pool-cleaning shirts in the van?"

109

"Those old disguises?" Joe said.

"They'll be perfect." Bending low, Frank made his way to the back of the van. He found the shirts wadded up in a box. The words Perfect Pools was written on top of the shirt pocket.

Frank handed a shirt to Joe.

"Phew." Joe wrinkled his nose. "These smell as if *they* could use a dunk in the pool."

But Frank was too busy rummaging in the van to hear him. With a triumphant grin he pulled out two large plastic bottles filled with liquid.

"But that stuff is for the radiator," Joe said, pointing to one jug. "And that other stuff is what Aunt Gertrude asked us to pick up to clean the floors."

"So keep the labels turned away. We'll go to the back door like all hired help."

Joe was doubtful that his brother's plan would work, but he didn't have any better ideas.

They climbed back into the front of the van, pulled into the drive, and drove around to the rear of the mansion. A young blond woman wearing a maid's uniform and apron answered the door.

"Yes? What do you want?" she asked with a strong foreign accent.

"We're here to clean the pool," Frank said.

The woman looked confused. Joe pointed to the pool, then showed her the bottle he held. "Clean. Pool," he repeated.

110

"Ah! Yes!" Understanding lighted her eyes. "Please do," she said, smiling.

Joe followed Frank to the kidney-shaped pool. There was a small waterfall at one end and a diving board at the other. Joe set down the plastic jug of floor cleaner. "So what now?"

"We try to get a look inside the house." Frank motioned to a sliding glass door on the far side of the pool. "Let's head over that way."

Frank started around the pool clockwise, and Joe walked in the other direction. Occasionally he stooped and stuck his finger in the water as if testing it.

When he reached the glass doors, Joe stepped closer and peered inside.

"See anybody?" Frank asked from behind him.

"Not yet," Joe said. "Wait. I think there's somebody in the next room. It looks like an office of some kind."

Suddenly there was the soft sound of footsteps behind the Hardys. Joe spun around. He and Frank were face to face with a gorilla in a three-piece suit.

"You kids better have a good reason for being here," the huge man growled. "Or you've just peeped in your last window!"

12 The Clue in the Photograph

"Uh, we're cleaning the pool," Frank stammered. He pointed to the label on his shirt. "We asked the maid for permission."

The guy stepped closer and towered over the two Hardys. Joe thought he looked as if he was wider than a door. Frank gulped, realizing the two of them wouldn't stand a chance if the apeman got mad.

"The maid doesn't speak English," the thug explained in a sarcastic voice.

"But she told us to clean the pool," Joe said, inching closer to Frank.

"Shut up, kid," snapped the bodyguard. He had curly black hair and a dark beard. A bulge

112

under his jacket made Frank suspect that he was carrying a gun. "Now, why don't you two come inside and ask the owner of the house if it's all right to clean the pool."

"That won't be necessary," Frank said quickly. "We'll come back another time. We're running really late for our next—"

The big guy grabbed Frank's arm, cutting off his explanation. "I didn't ask for your schedule. I said get inside, both of you."

The thug opened the sliding door, then ushered the two boys into the house and down a carpeted hallway. When they reached a doorway to the left, the man gestured for them to go in.

Frank looked around once he entered the room. A bookshelf filled with leather-bound books and sculptures covered one wall. Original paintings hung on another wall. At the far end of the room a large, elegantly dressed man sat behind a polished mahogany desk. Sitting across from him in an expensive-looking leather chair was Bill Harbison.

The man behind the desk smiled as the Hardys entered.

"I found these two pool boys outside, boss," the thug said. "They were peeping in the windows."

"Are these your young friends, Bill?" the man asked Harbison.

113

"Yeah," Harbison said, giving the Hardys a dirty look. "They've been bugging me for the last couple of days 'cause they think I know where Fred Hawkins is."

"And do you, Bill?" the man asked, raising an eyebrow. "You led me to believe that if you had the foggiest idea of Mr. Hawkins's whereabouts, you would have let me know."

Frank saw a frightened look cross Harbison's face.

"Of course I would," Harbison said nervously. "You *know* I'd tell you. I'd like to see Fred Hawkins show up every bit as much as you would."

"I should imagine you would," the man said, putting his hands together in front of him to make a steeple. "After all, it was *my* money that you were loaning Mr. Hawkins. And if he can't be made to pay his debt, then you'll have to come up with the money some other way."

Harbison turned pale but said nothing. The elegantly dressed man turned back to the Hardys. "So why are you boys looking for Mr. Hawkins?" he asked. "Surely he doesn't owe *you* money."

"We're trying to rescue him from his alien kidnappers," Joe said in a cocky voice.

Frank shot his brother a look that said, *Shut up.* The well-spoken man in front of them was not fooling around.

"Mrs. Hawkins asked us to help find him," Frank explained.

"Ah. Very noble of you to take on the task," the man said. Then he looked more closely at Frank. "Wait a minute, I think I recognize you boys."

"Everybody does," Joe said. "We were recently on the front page of the *Gazette.*"

"No," the man said. "I don't read the paper. I have people who do that for me. But I *have* seen your picture. You're those detective brothers people talk about. The Harley brothers."

"Close enough," Frank said.

"So now you're tracking down Fred Hawkins? That's very nice. Of course, if you find him, you *will* tell me where he is, won't you?" The cool look the man leveled at the boys told Frank they had no choice.

"I'm sure it'll be in all the papers," Joe said.

"Probably," the man said. "But I want to hear about it before it hits the papers. Do you understand?"

Frank and Joe both nodded emphatically.

The man gestured toward the bodyguard. "Jack, please escort these gentlemen to their car." Then he swung his icy gaze back to the Hardys. "I trust you won't repeat this conversation to anyone."

Joe raised his right hand. "Scout's honor."

Frank glanced back at Harbison before the

115

thug, Jack, led them out of the office. Some color had returned to the loan shark's face, but he still looked pretty uncomfortable.

With arms folded in front of him, Jack waited while the two Hardys walked across the pool deck and climbed into their van. Joe waved and flashed a big smile as Frank drove off, but the guy's stern expression didn't change.

"Whew," Joe said, turning around in his seat. "That was a close one! I thought we were goners when that gorilla came up behind us at the window."

"I have a feeling it's Bill Harbison who's in serious trouble," Frank said.

"What do you mean?" Joe asked as his brother drove back toward town.

"Didn't you recognize that guy behind the desk?" Frank asked. "That was Amos Woodworth the Fourth, one of the biggest wholesale merchandisers in the Bayport area."

Joe shook his head. "Never heard of him."

"Oh, I forgot," Frank said. "If it isn't in the sports section, you don't know anything about it."

"Very funny," Joe said. "So what's the big deal about Amos the Fourth?"

"He's a multibillionaire importer and exporter," Frank explained as he steered the car onto the highway. "But the law's been after him for years because they think he's involved in smuggling. Only they've never been able to pin anything on him. He's got an army of lawyers who make sure his records are squeaky clean."

"So Woodworth is supplying Harbison with the money that he lends people. And if Fred Hawkins doesn't turn up soon and pay off his debt, Woodworth's going to take it out of Harbison's flesh."

"Right," Frank said.

"So that clears Harbison. There's no way Mr. Loan Shark would have kidnapped Hawkins," Joe added.

Frank chuckled. "I'd say it would be the worst thing Harbison could possibly do. Jack the Apeman back there looks as if he'd love to mess up somebody's face."

"So who does that leave?" Joe ran his fingers through his hair. "First we scratched the aliens, then Everson and Rodriguez, and now Harbison."

"What about Mr. Hawkins himself?" Frank asked. "Maybe he decided to skip town instead of paying up."

Joe thought for a second. "Except his UFO plan worked. Because of all the publicity, the Happy Burger is making money like crazy, so that will help him pay off his other debts. And I don't think he'd run out on his wife—not permanently, anyway."

"What if she's in on it with him?" Frank suggested. "Maybe they're going to get together in a couple of weeks and head for Brazil."

Suddenly he stepped on the brakes, then made a sharp right turn. "I think we'll just talk to Clarissa Hawkins. She seemed genuinely upset about her husband's disappearance. But who knows? She might be the greatest actress in the world."

Fifteen minutes later Frank parked in front of a modest two-story home in the middle of a new development.

Joe pointed to the freshly seeded lawn. "Looks as though they just moved in."

"And I bet the mortgage added to Fred's money nightmares," Frank said as he climbed out of the van.

When the brothers reached the front stoop, Joe rang the bell. Seconds later Clarissa Hawkins opened the door. She was wearing a chef's apron that had flour smudges all over it.

From the startled expression on her face, Frank knew they were the last people she expected to see.

"Well, hello." She gave them a guarded smile. "The Hardy brothers, right?"

Frank nodded. "We wanted to keep you up to date on what we've discovered about your husband," he said.

"Of course," she said. Backing up, she swung open the door. "You'll have to excuse my appearance," she apologized. She brushed away a strand of hair, leaving a trail of flour across her forehead. "But I bake cookies for a living, and I have an order of twelve dozen to finish up."

Joe's face brightened. "Cookies!" He sniffed the air. "Smells like gingerbread."

Clarissa Hawkins smiled openly for the first time. "Gingersnaps. You see them in all the specialty stores. Would you boys like to sample them? I always have a plate of rejects."

"Sounds great," Frank said as they followed her into her kitchen.

After the boys settled on two kitchen chairs, Frank began to tell Mrs. Hawkins about Fred's kidnapping scheme. Since Mrs. Hawkins was dropping rounded teaspoonsful of dough onto a cookie sheet, being careful to keep them at least two inches apart, he couldn't tell what her reaction was.

"So now he's really disappeared, and we're stumped. Which is one reason why we came to you," Frank finished up.

"Is there anything you can tell us that might help us find Fred this time?" Joe asked.

"Well, I——" Mrs. Hawkins stammered. Suddenly she started to sob. Frank and Joe rolled their eyes at each other. Not again!

"Are you all right?" Frank asked when her sobs had quieted. He reached across the kitchen table and handed her a napkin.

119

She nodded and dabbed her eyes. "It's just that these have been the worst few days of my life. Policemen, reporters, nosy people who drive up and ring my doorbell. And all because of Fred's stupid UFO scheme. And now he's *really* missing!"

"So you knew all about the first so-called kidnapping," Joe said.

"Not at first." She blew her nose. "He finally called me late last night and told me what he'd done. And I told him it was the craziest idea he'd ever had." Finally she looked up at them. "And believe me, Fred's had some crazy ideas. Starting the Happy Burger was the first down-to-earth project he's ever followed through on. So when I found out from you two how much money he'd borrowed to do it, I almost died."

"So he hadn't told you about William Harbison and the twenty thousand dollars," Frank said.

She sighed and shook her head no. "Last night he told me the UFO thing was to generate publicity for the restaurant. If I'd known about the money, I probably would've convinced him to do something more realistic. We could've sold the house and moved into something smaller," she added in a resigned voice. Then her eyes snapped with determination. "But this time I know something really *has* happened to Fred. The whole plan was supposed to be over today—

he told me so last night. You boys will stay on the case, won't you?"

"Of course," Frank replied.

For a second the room was quiet except for the sound of Joe crunching gingersnaps. "So who does that leave for us to investigate?" Joe finally asked as he reached for another cookie. "The UFO Brigade?"

Frank shrugged. "What's their motive? They showed up to check out the kidnapping, not cause it. They just want to meet the aliens."

"Wait a minute," Mrs. Hawkins suddenly cut in. "There *is* something that might help. It's not much, but when I went to the Happy Burger while Sandra Rodriguez was doing her broadcast, I recognized someone. I didn't expect him to be there."

"Who?" Frank asked excitedly, hoping it was the break they'd been looking for.

Wiping her hands on her apron, Clarissa left the room. Seconds later she came back with a large framed photo in her hand.

"This was taken at the officers' reunion that Fred and I went to a few months ago," she explained.

Standing up, Frank and Joe looked over her shoulder. The photo was of a posed group of about thirty men and women dressed in uniform.

Mrs. Hawkins scanned the picture, then

121

pointed to a tall man in the middle. "He's the man who helped my husband with the UFO stunt."

Excited, Frank looked where she was pointing. Then his heart sank. It was Matt Everson.

"Yeah. We know him," Frank explained, trying to keep the disappointment out of his voice.

"Then that won't help you?" Mrs. Hawkins asked, her eyes brimming with tears again.

"No. But I found something that will!" Joe exclaimed. "Look who else was at the reunion." He pointed to a stocky guy with a grim expression. "Our Brigader friend, Carl Thurmon!"

13 Operation Rescue

"Thurmon!" Frank took the photo from Mrs. Hawkins and studied it. "You're right! Hodding Wheatley said Carl Thurmon was in Vietnam. I didn't realize he'd been an officer."

"Do you remember that guy?" Joe pointed the Brigader out to Mrs. Hawkins.

"Yes. As a matter of fact, he hung around a lot." She shuddered. "I thought he was weird, but Fred told me to ignore him, that he was just a little 'off' because of an accident during the war."

Frank and Joe flashed each other excited grins.

"Are you thinking what I'm thinking?" Joe asked his brother.

Frank nodded. "I think Thurmon must've

heard snatches of UFO talk between Everson and Mr. Hawkins when they were at the reunion. Thurmon must have arrived in Bayport expecting a real UFO sighting. Then he found out Mr. Hawkins was somehow involved."

"Maybe he saw his photo in the *Bayport Gazette,*" Joe suggested.

"Right. And Thurmon instantly realized the whole thing was a hoax," Frank said. "It must have made him furious."

"And we know how Thurmon gets when he's furious," Joe added.

Mrs. Hawkins looked confused. "I still don't understand why Mr. Thurmon would kidnap Fred."

Joe shrugged. "Probably the only person who can answer that question is Thurmon himself."

Frank handed the photo back to Mrs. Hawkins. "Which means we'd better find him," he said, heading toward the door.

"Shouldn't you call the police?" Mrs. Hawkins called after them.

Joe waved over his shoulder. "We will, but right now, we've got to move fast!"

Twenty minutes later Frank zoomed into the parking lot of the shopping center.

"There's one of the Brigaders' vans." Joe pointed to the left of the Happy Burger. It was late afternoon, the crowd had thinned, and there was no sign of Sandra Rodriguez's crew.

"Don't tell me all the excitement's died down already," Frank said.

"I see there're still some serious UFOlogists lurking around," Joe said as Frank pulled in next to the Brigaders' van.

Joe jumped out before their van even stopped. He recognized a familiar redhead sitting on the curb. Dan Hoffman was looking at a map, which he had spread out on his lap.

"Where's Carl Thurmon?" Joe demanded, striding up to him.

Startled, Hoffman jumped up. He wore his silver suit under a leather flight jacket. "What do you want him for?"

"Because we think he kidnapped Fred Hawkins," Joe said.

Just then Frank joined his brother. Dan Hoffman glanced back and forth at the two of them. At the same time three other Brigaders silently came up behind Hoffman.

"I don't know anything about it," Hoffman replied in a stern voice.

Joe snatched the map from the man's hand and waved it in his face. "I think you do. I think you know Thurmon has Mr. Hawkins, but you're too scared to tell anyone. After all, the police already think you're a bunch of troublemakers."

Frank took the map from Joe. "What's this you have circled?" he asked Hoffman.

"We don't have to tell you anything," one of the Brigaders behind Hoffman said. With an angry scowl the man moved toward Joe.

Dan Hoffman raised his hand swiftly to stop him. "We'd better tell these guys," he said to the others. "They may be our only chance to get to Carl."

Taking a deep breath, Hoffman turned back to Frank and Joe. "You're right. Carl's got Fred. Only Thurmon said if we tried anything, he'd kill him. That's why we haven't made a move."

"But why would he kill Mr. Hawkins?" Frank asked.

Hoffman shook his head wearily. "I'm afraid Thurmon's finally snapped. He told us Fred was the head of a conspiracy to fool the world by sending a false message from the aliens. At first we didn't pay any attention to him. But when Sandra Rodriguez showed up and planned that obviously contrived landing in Bayport Meadows, we knew something was up. But then it was too late."

"You mean Thurmon snatched Hawkins when he was at Bayport Meadows?" Frank guessed.

Hoffman nodded. "Carl was a communications expert in Vietnam. He managed to bug the room and tap the phone at the motel where Rodriguez was staying. He must've heard enough of their plans to figure out that Matt Everson was leaving Fred Hawkins in Bayport Meadows early in the morning."

"So he snuck up and snatched him while it was still dark," Joe concluded. "That note Fred left must've *really* been a cry for help!"

"Why didn't you tell anyone?" Frank demanded.

Hoffman spread his hands in a helpless gesture. "Because we weren't positive that Carl had really done anything until about an hour ago."

"I'm not sure I believe these guys." Joe turned to Frank. "Remember we saw Thurmon at Bayport Meadows, and he was communicating with them via walkie-talkie."

"Thurmon showed up to tell us that Fred Hawkins wasn't going to appear," Hoffman explained. "When it turned out he was right, we immediately interrogated him. All he would tell us was that *he* was now in charge of things, that the 'alien hoax' was coming to an end. Then he managed to get away—he'd brought his own jeep to Bayport—and we lost him."

Frank frowned at the Brigader. "You mean you don't know where he is?"

Hoffman took the map from Frank and pointed to the circle he'd drawn. "The group has a cabin in the woods outside Bayport. It's kind of a survivalist camp. We assume that's where Carl took Hawkins. We haven't taken action because, as I told you before, Carl said that if we interfered in any way, he'd make sure Fred Hawkins *never* talked."

"What do you think Thurmon is planning to do with Hawkins?" Joe asked.

"Our guess is he's trying to brainwash him into believing the *real* alien message—at least the message that Carl thinks the world should hear. If Hawkins is smart, he'll cooperate and Thurmon will let him go."

"And if Hawkins resists?" Frank asked.

Hoffman shrugged. "There's no telling what Thurmon will do," he said grimly.

Joe and Frank exchanged glances.

"Which means we've got to get Hawkins out of there," Joe said. "And quickly."

Frank nodded. "And I think I've got a plan." He turned back to Hoffman. "You guys had better get to the police and convince them you're not *all* loony. We may need backup. Can we take the map?"

When Hoffman nodded, Frank took it from the Brigader. Clapping Joe on the shoulder, he headed for their van. "Come on, little brother, I'll explain my plan on the way. We need to pick up Hodding Wheatley."

They found the author eating dinner in the diner next to the motel where he'd told them he was staying. When Joe and Frank sat down on either side of Wheatley, he looked at them with cool curiosity.

"Somehow I don't think you're joining me for dinner," Mr. Wheatley said.

Joe waved at the waitress. "Actually, a big, juicy steak and a baked potato would taste great."

"All we have time for is a takeout sandwich," Frank reminded his brother. After they'd ordered, Frank and Joe explained all that had happened that day. As the Hardys talked, Mr. Wheatley's eyes grew larger and larger.

"So Hawkins engineered the whole hoax," Wheatley said with wonder. "He must be a clever fellow."

"Not that clever." Joe snorted. "After all, he got caught by Carl Thurmon."

Mr. Wheatley dabbed his mouth, then folded his napkin and placed it on the table. "So what can I do to help?"

"I think you're probably the only guy Thurmon will trust," Frank said. "I'm going to drive you to the cabin. You approach Thurmon on your own. Once you've gained his trust, tell him you've heard that he's holding someone who's received a message from the aliens. Tell him you've brought a cameraman to record the story so you can tell it to the world."

"We've got a Camcorder back at our house— we'll pick it up on the way to the cabin," Joe added. Then he frowned at Frank. "You think he won't remember you? I mean, you were there when he tried to knock me out with that little UFO of his."

"I stayed in the background. Besides, he never really knew we were investigating," Frank explained. "Maybe he'll accept Wheatley's explanation that I'm a cameraman, even if I *was* hanging out with you."

"Maybe," Joe muttered. "Though I guess we don't have much choice. Every second we spend waiting puts Fred Hawkins in that much more danger."

"Exactly," Frank said. "Which is why we've got to move right now."

Hodding Wheatley stood up. "Then let's go." He hesitated for a second. "But what do we do after we get into the cabin? I'm an author, not an undercover cop."

Frank smiled. "That's where Joe comes in, with plan B. He'll be working on his own. I'll explain the trick I've got up my sleeve on the way to the cabin."

"And if Frank's plan fails, the police will be arriving for backup," Joe said.

An hour later Frank drove the van up a bumpy lane in the middle of the woods. Hodding Wheatley sat in the passenger seat. It was shortly after dark, and the forest was filled with eerie shadows.

"You think we took a wrong turn?" Wheatley asked in a nervous voice.

Frank shook his head. "There weren't any turns. But it's true, this road doesn't seem to be going anywhere."

Just then the van bounced into a clearing. Frank cut the lights and quickly shut off the engine. A sliver of moon peeped over the trees, silhouetting several dark shapes in the distance.

"That must be where Thurmon's holding Hawkins." Frank pointed to the largest building. A dim light, probably produced by a battery-powered lantern, was visible through the cabin window.

Wheatley took a deep breath. "Well, let's go." As the pair quietly climbed out from the van and approached the cabin door, Hodding Wheatley turned and gave Frank a questioning look, as if to make sure that he really wanted to go ahead with the plan.

Frank nodded to indicate that he did. Then he held his finger to his lips. He wanted to check out the cabin before going in. It might be smart to find out if there was another exit—just in case.

Leaving Wheatley by the front steps, Frank circled around to a side window. It was low enough so he could easily peek in. He flattened himself against the side of the cabin, then slowly leaned toward the window to look in.

He saw a bunk bed against the back wall and a doorway that appeared to lead to a bathroom or closet. Leaning even closer to the window, Frank saw Fred Hawkins. He was sitting bound and gagged on a chair against one wall. Carl Thurmon stood over him, a crazed expression on his face, and he was gripping something in his hand.

Frank had to force himself not to gasp. The Brigader was holding a hunting knife, and the sharp blade was aimed at Fred's throat!

14 Cabin Fever

Quickly Frank ran from the window toward the front of the house. He passed Wheatley and, without saying a word, rushed up the steps of the front porch.

"Mr. Thurmon," he called in as calm a voice as he could muster, hoping the sound would stop the Brigader from hurting Hawkins.

Frank knocked lightly on the door, then gestured for Wheatley to come onto the porch.

"Mr. Thurmon," the author chimed in. "It's Hodding Wheatley. I hear you're holding an important witness. I'd like to talk to you."

For what seemed like forever, there was no reply. Then Carl Thurmon opened the door a crack and peered out. Frank stepped back into the shadows. The Brigader, in his silver suit, was still holding the hunting knife in his hand, and Frank didn't want to provoke him.

Thurmon looked at Wheatley with a puzzled frown. "Hey! I know you." His expression changed when he recognized the author. "You really *are* Hodding Wheatley."

Wheatley nodded. "Yes. Your friends the Brigaders sent me. They said you and Fred Hawkins had received an important message from the aliens. I'm here to help you spread that message to the world."

Thurmon thought a moment, as if considering Wheatley's words. "Well, *I've* got an important message. Hawkins here says he'll join me, but I'm not so sure he's a true believer." He grinned nastily. "Only I think maybe I can convince him."

"Perhaps you should let me talk to Mr. Hawkins," Wheatley said in his most persuasive voice. "After all, we don't want to hurt someone who's met with the aliens."

Frank held his breath, hoping Thurmon would accept Wheatley's explanation. Frank and Wheatley had agreed not to let on to Thurmon that they knew the whole UFO thing was a hoax.

"Okay." Stepping aside, Carl Thurmon opened the cabin door wider. But when he saw Frank standing next to Wheatley, he glared angrily at the author and barred the way with his arm.

"Why did you bring him?" he growled. "Are you trying to trick me?"

Wheatley held up his hand in a gesture of peace. Frank noticed that it was shaking.

"It's all right," Wheatley said gently. "This young man is on our side. He's my cameraman."

"Cameraman! He's one of the guys who hassled me yesterday at the shopping center!"

"We just didn't know you were on our side," Frank said. "My partner even thought you might be a government agent. You were awfully suspicious of everyone." Carl Thurmon still looked skeptical.

"How did we know *you* weren't a phony?" Frank added.

"A phony?" Carl Thurmon looked genuinely upset. "I've been dedicated to the cause all my life. But you've got to understand. I have been betrayed time after time by others who did not truly believe. The entire UFO Brigade betrayed me this very afternoon. Besides"—Thurmon smirked—"I knew once I saw Fred Hawkins's picture in the paper that the UFO sighting was phony."

Frank and Wheatley both tried to look shocked.

"A—a phony?" Wheatley stammered. "But how can that be?"

"Hawkins thought the whole thing up with that stupid talk show host and her sidekick, Matt

135

Everson," Thurmon said. "I was on to them like a flash, though," he added proudly.

"Why, those creeps!" Frank declared with exaggerated anger. "Now I can understand your suspicion and lack of trust."

With a nod Thurmon threw the door open wide and stepped back. With the sharp tip of his knife, he gestured toward Hawkins. "And that jerk was the ringleader," he growled. "I told him I'd let him go if he vowed to join me in my quest to bring the alien message to the world."

"And did he agree?" Wheatley asked.

"Yeah. But I don't think he really means it. Right, Fred?" Leaning closer, Thurmon sneered in the other man's face.

With wild, frightened eyes Fred Hawkins glanced at Frank, then at Hodding Wheatley. Frank would have liked to assure the man they were on his side, but he knew he couldn't respond in any way that might tip off Thurmon. He only hoped Hawkins remembered him from that evening at the Happy Burger.

Frank quickly glanced around the cabin. He noted grimly that other than the front door and the narrow window, there was no way to escape. The cabin was sparsely furnished with just the necessities. In the small kitchenette there was a pump handle over the sink. Thurmon had set up a kerosene stove to heat food. Several open cans lay

136

scattered on the counter. There was a fireplace, with wood stacked beside it.

In the middle of the room was a small hand-made table and two chairs. Next to it a portable television had been placed on a stool. Frank figured it operated by batteries since there were no electrical outlets in the room. It was tuned to a local news broadcast. Thurmon must have turned the volume down, since there was no sound coming from it. Frank thought that later he'd find a reason to turn it up, in order to mask the sound of the arriving police.

When Frank turned back to Thurmon and Wheatley, the author was stooped down, talking to Fred Hawkins.

"Mr. Hawkins," Wheatley was saying in his melodious voice, "we know you must be on our side. Only a genius with great knowledge and interest in UFOs could have built such a convincing ship. Will you join us?"

Fred Hawkins nodded emphatically.

Frank moved toward the back of Hawkins's chair. "If I take off your gag, will you promise not to scream?"

Carl Thurmon chuckled. "Not that it'll do any good way out here. I just got sick of listening to him rattle on and on about how he didn't want me to hurt him." Thurmon slapped his knife against the palm of his hand. "I told him I only

137

hurt people who get in the way of my message. Like government stooges." He glared at Frank as if he still wasn't absolutely convinced by his story.

Frank tried to ignore the man's angry look. "There." He untied the handkerchief gag.

"Thank you!" Fred gasped. "It was getting hard to swallow."

Wheatley put his hands on Hawkins's bound ones. "Now. We're here to talk about the true alien message," he said with false sincerity. "Will you help us send it to the world?"

"Oh, yes!" Hawkins agreed readily. He cast nervous eyes toward Thurmon. "In my quest to build the perfect UFO, I learned much that will help spread knowledge to all unbelievers."

Frank nodded. Good. Hawkins had caught on to what he and Wheatley were trying to do.

Thurmon gestured toward Frank's camcorder. "So what do you plan to do with that toy?" he asked in a suspicious tone.

"The TV news programs use tapes made on these things all the time," Frank replied. "And since we didn't think you'd want a whole camera crew stomping through your hideout, Wheatley thought this would be best."

"Okay." Thurmon put his knife in its sheath, which was underneath his belt. "So let's get down to the interview. It's about time someone asked *me* about UFOs. After all, I'm one of the few people who have really communicated with aliens. Other than you, Mr. Wheatley," he said respectfully.

Frank picked up the camera. Hodding Wheatley pulled a chair from under the table and sat down.

"Ladies and gentlemen," he started when Frank turned on the camera, "my name is Hodding Wheatley and today I bring you—"

"Wait a minute!" Carl Thurmon's gruff voice cut him off. "I want to hear what that stupid TV lady has to say." He strode to the television and turned up the volume.

Frank looked over to see Sandra Rodriguez on the screen. She wore a serious expression, as though she was about to impart an extremely important piece of news.

Frank's stomach fell. He had a terrible feeling the talk show host was going to say something that would blow their cover.

"Uh, Mr. Thurmon, don't you think we'd better get on with this interview?" Frank asked, walking toward the TV.

Reaching out his arm, Thurmon blocked his way. "If you touch that dial, I'll slice your fingers off," he growled.

Frank backed up. "On the other hand, I guess we can wait."

"This is Sandra Rodriguez in Bayport," the interviewer said. "There's been an important development in the Bayport UFO kidnapping case—a development that completely alters the complexion of the whole affair. It has been revealed that the kidnapping was in fact a *hoax*. And that the hoax was entirely engineered by the kidnapping victim himself, Fred Hawkins!"

A picture of Hawkins appeared on the screen.

Carl Thurmon chuckled. "So the big lady is finally admitting the truth. It's about time."

"Only it's not the whole truth," Fred Hawkins said in a disgusted tone. "They were as much a part of it as I was."

Sandra Rodriguez continued, "The true story of the kidnapping was uncovered this afternoon by a pair of brave local detectives, dedicated to revealing that such UFO sightings are nothing more than deliberate efforts to deceive the public. These detectives, brothers not yet out of high school, are Frank and Joe Hardy."

Pictures of Frank and Joe, which Frank recognized from his high school yearbook, flashed side by side on the screen.

Thurmon spun around, a look of such rage on his face that Frank's sinking feeling turned into one of terror. Grabbing Wheatley's arm, Frank pulled the author off the chair and shoved him toward the door.

"Run for it!" he yelled, and Wheatley took off.

"You're a detective?" Thurmon yanked the knife out of its sheath and brandished it in the air. "I thought I smelled a rat. I should have trusted my instincts. You are not a true believer of the cause at all. In fact, I bet you're part of the hoax."

Footsteps clattering on the wooden porch told Frank that Hodding Wheatley had gotten away. Thurmon didn't even seem to notice. His face was purple with rage. The veins bulged on his temples, and his fingers were clutching the knife handle so tightly that his knuckles had turned white.

"Hey, let's not jump to conclusions here," Frank said quickly. "You know how these stories get distorted by the news media."

Raising the video camera, Frank held it in front of him like a shield. He wished he could make a run for it, too. But there was no way he was going to leave Fred Hawkins alone with this madman.

Thurmon raised his knife, and the blade glinted in the light of the lantern. Swallowing hard, Frank stepped backward.

"There's only one thing to do with traitors like you and Hawkins," Thurmon said, advancing menacingly on Frank. "They must be eliminated so they can never betray the cause again!"

141

15 The Great
UFO Scam

Carl Thurmon lunged at Frank with the knife. Frank dodged sideways, and the blade sliced wildly through the air.

"Hey," Frank said in a bantering tone, hoping he might be able to distract the Brigader. "You really don't need to use that thing on a friend. I mean, somebody might get hurt."

"We are not friends," Thurmon retorted. He relaxed the hand holding the knife blade. Seeing his chance, Frank hit the knife with the video camera. The lens caught the tip of the blade, jarring it loose from Thurmon's grasp. Then, suddenly, the Brigader cried out as he began to pitch forward.

Frank glanced down to see Hawkins's outstretched legs. They'd caught Thurmon's ankles. The Brigader flew forward, knocking his head on the edge of the table as he fell to the floor.

Cautiously Frank inched toward the man and prodded him with his toe. Thurmon was out cold.

"Thanks, Mr. Hawkins." Frank breathed a sigh of relief as he kicked the knife into the ashes of the fireplace. "Now let's get out of here. I don't want to be anywhere around when that lunatic comes to."

Frank moved to Fred's chair, then bent down to try and loosen the skillfully tied knots. Suddenly he heard a sound behind him. He twisted around, but it was too late. A chair came crashing down on his head. Moaning, Frank sank to the floor.

Carl Thurmon stood over him, a crazed gleam in his eyes. "You should've paid closer attention, kid." He chuckled. "One hit on this hard head's not going to stop me. But this is going to stop *you!*" He held up the lantern and some newspaper.

Frank rubbed the back of his neck. It felt damp, and when he looked at his fingers, they were smeared with blood. He tried to jump up to kick the lantern from Thurmon's hand, but his legs buckled under him.

"Look, Thurmon," Fred Hawkins said from the

143

chair, "this thing is all my fault. I'll pay for my sins. Frank's just a kid. And you can see he's hurt. Why don't you let him go?"

But Thurmon ignored him. He was busy crumpling up the newspaper. "The aliens will understand why I acted as I did. And when the reporters get here, all they'll find is your charred bodies. Of course, I'll be in another state by then. They'll blame the fire on a faulty lantern."

"Only Mr. Wheatley's going to be here with the cops any minute," Frank said, his words coming out haltingly.

Thurmon snorted. "Wheatley won't get a mile before I catch him."

Frank tried to sit up. His shoulders ached where the chair had cracked across his back, and he was seeing two Thurmons. If only Joe would hurry up and get here, he thought. What was taking him so long?

Thurmon unscrewed the plug in the lantern, then began to sprinkle kerosene on the paper, which was all over the floor. Next he pulled a cigarette lighter from his pocket.

Frank struggled to his feet. "Hey, look, Mr. Thurmon," he said desperately. He was extremely dizzy, however, and he lost his balance, falling back to the floor. But he knew he had to do something, even if it was just stalling the Brigader. "Don't you think the aliens are going to be angry that you're killing innocent humans to spread their message? I bet they're flying around out there right now, watching your every move. Right, Mr. Hawkins?"

"Right," he said, with equal desperation. "The aliens wouldn't want you to hurt us. I mean, I only wanted to drum up business for my restaurant and get out of debt. I never meant you or your friends in outer space any harm."

"Shut up, you two," Thurmon snapped. "You don't know anything. If the aliens are out there, it's because they want to congratulate me on eliminating unbelievers." He held a rolled-up piece of newspaper to the lighter, and it caught fire.

Just then a whistling, whirring noise echoed through the cabin. Frank glanced toward the window. A strange blue light filled the clearing outside. Dropping the burning newspaper, Carl Thurmon rushed to the window and looked out.

"I don't believe it! The aliens have heard my call!" he exclaimed. He spun around and dashed out the open front door. Frank watched the flickering flames as the paper began to burn more brightly and spread around the cabin.

Next to him, Hawkins struggled in his chair, and Frank realized he'd better do something— fast. The fire had spread too rapidly for Frank to try to control it. He decided it would be quicker to free Hawkins.

"We've got to get out of here," Hawkins said. "This place is a tinderbox."

Holding his pounding head with one hand, Frank inched toward the chair. With fumbling movements he untied Hawkins. The man rubbed his hands and wrists, then helped Frank to his feet.

"You take it easy. The back of your head's bleeding," he told Frank.

With Hawkins's help Frank made his way toward the door. He could feel the heat of the flames as they spread quickly along the line of newspapers and up the walls. The inside of the cabin seemed to glow, and when they reached the door, he had to blink several times before his eyes could adjust to the dark.

"What in the world!" Hawkins stopped dead on the porch. In the middle of the clearing a UFO was touching down. A ring of blue lights blinked on and off, and the whistling noise was deafening.

Almost underneath it Carl Thurmon was standing frozen. He was staring up at the strange sight, his arms raised as if he were about to embrace it.

Frank grinned. "Thank goodness." He sighed. "The aliens have finally landed."

Inside the UFO Joe yanked twice on the dangling rope, the signal to Matt Everson to land.

146

With a soft thud the flying saucer settled on the ground. Quickly Joe scrambled to the hatch on the side of the saucer. He had no idea what he would find when he opened the door. Would his brother be safe? Or was he too late?

Joe opened the door, stuck out his head, and looked around. The blue lights illuminated the area enough so he could see Carl Thurmon standing about ten feet away. The man's eyes were filled with awe, until he swung his gaze to Joe.

Startled, the Brigader didn't react for a second. Then he lunged toward Joe.

"He's got a knife!" Joe heard Frank yell. With lightning reflexes Joe leapt to the ground. Landing lightly on his feet, he faced the furious man.

"You're that other Hardy!" Thurmon yelled as he advanced toward Joe.

"That's me," Joe said. Without another word Thurmon lunged at him with the knife. Joe kicked forward. His foot caught Thurmon's wrist. With a cry of pain, the Brigader dropped the knife. Joe landed another kick to the man's midsection. The force propelled Thurmon backward, and he fell with a crash.

At the same time a new set of lights appeared in the sky. They were the lights of a helicopter descending almost on top of the flying saucer. Only a thin black cable, nearly invisible in the darkness, connected the saucer with the chopper above.

At the last second the helicopter changed course and landed next to the saucer. Out climbed Sandra Rodriguez, followed a moment later by Matt Everson.

"Wow! What a way to get an exclusive!" Sandra Rodriguez gasped when she saw Thurmon flat on the ground.

Joe felt like slugging her. But finding out if his brother was all right was more important.

He sprinted toward the cabin. Flames were leaping up the dry wooden walls and onto the ceiling. Any second the whole place could blow up.

Then Joe saw Frank and Fred Hawkins making their way slowly across the clearing. Hawkins was supporting Frank.

"Are you all right?" Joe asked, running up to his brother.

"I've been better," Frank said, grimacing in pain.

Just then more lights flashed in their eyes as two police cars roared up the dirt drive. When the first one stopped, Hodding Wheatley jumped from the patrol car.

"I met the police about a mile down the road," he explained breathlessly. "We got here as fast as we could." His eyes fastened on Frank. "Thank goodness you're all right! That was a brave thing you did back there."

"You're telling me," Hawkins chimed in. "He saved both our lives."

Joe slipped his arm under his brother's shoulders to help support him. "That's my brother," he said proudly.

Frank smiled back at him. "Hey. Thanks to you and Matt, too. If it wasn't for you and that UFO, we would've been cooked well done by now. Thurmon didn't recognize me at first, just like we hoped. But then he saw our pictures on the news—and it put him over the top."

Turning, Joe stared at the burning cabin. The walls collapsed with a crash. Just then the police led Carl Thurmon to the patrol car. Sandra Rodriguez ran alongside the Brigader.

"And do you still think the aliens will communicate with you?" she was asking in a dramatic voice.

Joe chuckled. "Think we should finally give her the privilege of interviewing us?" he asked.

"Sure," Frank replied. "Only let's make sure she gets our names right!"

The smell of hamburgers rose from the kitchen of the Happy Burger. Frank smiled as Chet Morton placed two plates of burgers and fries on the counter in front of him and Joe.

"Compliments of the house," Chet said.

"I think we earned it," Joe said. He was sitting next to Iola. On the other side of him sat Frank, Callie, and Hodding Wheatley. Frank had a square gauze bandage on the back of his head. He had been taken to the emergency room, where he was examined and x-rayed. Fortunately the cut hadn't been deep enough to require stitches. A good night's sleep had put him right back in shape. "What do *you* think, Frank?" Joe asked.

"I think we've earned a lifetime subscription to these things," he said. "All the hamburgers we can eat."

Chet placed a plate heaped with fries and a juicy burger in front of Hodding Wheatley.

The author stared at it for a moment. "Uh, you wouldn't by any chance have something low in cholesterol?" he asked politely.

The group burst out laughing.

Fred Hawkins, who was standing next to his wife, Clarissa, beamed at the Hardys. "You've got it, boys," he said. "You'll never have to pay for a hamburger at the Happy Burger as long as I'm the owner."

"Which should be for a pretty long time," Joe said. "Now that business has turned around."

"Right," Mrs. Hawkins said. Smiling, she surveyed the crowd of people in the restaurant. "I'm still furious at Fred for staging that flying saucer hoax and worrying me nearly to death. But it really did bring a lot of people into the restaurant."

Hawkins draped an arm around his wife's shoulders, then nodded toward Chet. "And most of them stuck around, thanks to Chet Morton and his UFO burgers. I have to admit, I didn't realize what a talented cook you were until now, Chet."

"Ah, shucks, it's nothing," Chet said.

Louise came up beside Chet and clapped him on the shoulder. "My co-worker is much too modest. Not only can he flip a great burger, but he works like a slave to make sure all the customers leave satisfied."

Chet grinned sheepishly. "You work just as hard, Louise."

"So how are you coming, paying off your debt, Mr. Hawkins?" Frank asked. "Now that you've got a successful restaurant."

"Well, I'm no longer making the payments to Mr. Harbison. After I told the police about our loan arrangement, they investigated his business and discovered a few irregularities, if you know what I mean. They're going to go after a Mr. Woodworth, too, who was apparently backing Harbison's loan-sharking operation."

"Will wonders never cease?" Joe chuckled.

"Plus, our lawyer is arranging to have the debt

transferred to a legitimate bank," Clarissa Hawkins added. "That should improve our interest rate considerably."

"So what's going to happen to Sandra Rodriguez and her boyfriend, Matt Everson?" Callie asked.

Hawkins shook his head. "Nothing. I signed a statement saying she and the show couldn't be held liable, and since Matt helped rescue me, I feel I owe him one."

"And now she wants us all to be on her talk show," Joe added with a grin.

Louise, Iola, and Callie squealed together.

"Oooh—can we come to the studio and watch?" Callie asked.

Joe flashed the three girls a smug look. "Sure. But remember, I don't do autographs."

"And what about the UFO Brigade?" Fred asked. "Anybody know what happened to them?"

"They quietly packed up and left before anyone could question them," Hodding Wheatley replied. "I think they'll probably keep a very low profile for a while."

"As for Mr. Thurmon," Frank added, "he's being charged with kidnapping and assault with a deadly weapon. He should be in prison for a long time."

Clarissa Hawkins patted her husband's arm. "Thank goodness the district attorney has decided not to press charges against Fred. They told him he had to make a public apology. It will appear on the front page of tomorrow's *Bayport Gazette*."

"Uh-oh," Chet said suddenly. "We'd better prepare for another mob of customers, Louise." He sighed deeply.

"What's the matter, Chet?" Frank asked. His friend was staring down morosely at a plate of burgers and fries. "Everything ended happily ever after. Even Mr. Wheatley's made out. He's decided to write a book called *The Great UFO Scam*."

Wheatley smiled modestly. "Only this book will be fiction," he said.

"That's nice, Mr. Wheatley," Chet said, but he still looked glum.

"Hey, and you've got the perfect job," Joe reminded his best friend. "One that lets you eat free hamburgers all day."

"Yeah, I guess," Chet said with a shrug. "But you know, I think I'm kind of, well, getting tired of hamburgers."

A laugh went up and down the counter.

"No, that's too incredible!" Joe said. Reaching over the counter, he clapped Chet on the shoulder. "Flying saucers, maybe! But Chet Morton getting sick of hamburgers? That's something that will *never* happen!"

NANCY DREW® MYSTERY STORIES By Carolyn Keene

☐ #57: THE TRIPLE HOAX	69153-8/$3.99	
☐ #58: THE FLYING SAUCER MYSTERY	72320-0/$3.50	
☐ #59: THE SECRET IN THE OLD LACE	69067-1/$3.99	
☐ #60: THE GREEK SYMBOL MYSTERY	67457-9/$3.50	
☐ #61: THE SWAMI'S RING	62467-9/$3.50	
☐ #62: THE KACHINA DOLL MYSTERY	67220-7/$3.99	
☐ #63: THE TWIN DILEMMA	67301-7/$3.99	
☐ #64: CAPTIVE WITNESS	70471-0/$3.50	
☐ #65: MYSTERY OF THE WINGED LION	62681-7/$3.50	
☐ #66: RACE AGAINST TIME	69485-5/$3.50	
☐ #67: THE SINISTER OMEN	73938-7/$3.50	
☐ #68: THE ELUSIVE HEIRESS	62478-4/$3.99	
☐ #69: CLUE IN THE ANCIENT DISGUISE	64279-0/$3.50	
☐ #70: THE BROKEN ANCHOR	74228-0/$3.50	
☐ #71: THE SILVER COBWEB	70992-5/$3.50	
☐ #72: THE HAUNTED CAROUSEL	66227-9/$3.50	
☐ #73: ENEMY MATCH	64283-9/$3.50	
☐ #74: MYSTERIOUS IMAGE	69401-4/$3.50	
☐ #75: THE EMERALD-EYED CAT MYSTERY	64282-0/$3.50	
☐ #76: THE ESKIMO'S SECRET	73003-7/$3.50	
☐ #77: THE BLUEBEARD ROOM	66857-9/$3.50	
☐ #78: THE PHANTOM OF VENICE	73422-9/$3.50	
☐ #79: THE DOUBLE HORROR OF FENLEY	64387-8/$3.99	
PLACE		
☐ #80: THE CASE OF THE DISAPPEARING	64896-9/$3.50	
DIAMONDS		
☐ #81: MARDI GRAS MYSTERY	64961-2/$3.99	
☐ #82: THE CLUE IN THE CAMERA	64962-0/$3.50	
☐ #83: THE CASE OF THE VANISHING VEIL	63413-5/$3.50	
☐ #84: THE JOKER'S REVENGE	63414-3/$3.50	
☐ #85: THE SECRET OF SHADY GLEN	63416-X/$3.50	
☐ #86: THE MYSTERY OF MISTY CANYON	63417-8/$3.99	

☐ #87: THE CASE OF THE RISING STARS	66312-7/$3.50
☐ #88: THE SEARCH FOR CINDY AUSTIN	66313-5/$3.50
☐ #89: THE CASE OF THE DISAPPEARING	66314-3/$3.50
DEEJAY	
☐ #90: THE PUZZLE AT PINEVIEW SCHOOL	66315-1/$3.95
☐ #91: THE GIRL WHO COULDN'T REMEMBER	66316-X/$3.50
☐ #92: THE GHOST OF CRAVEN COVE	66317-8/$3.50
☐ #93: THE CASE OF THE SAFECRACKER'S	66318-6/$3.50
SECRET	
☐ #94: THE PICTURE PERFECT MYSTERY	66315-1/$3.50
☐ #95: THE SILENT SUSPECT	69280-1/$3.50
☐ #96: THE CASE OF THE PHOTO FINISH	69281-X/$3.99
☐ #97: THE MYSTERY AT MAGNOLIA MANSION	69282-8/$3.99
☐ #98: THE HAUNTING OF HORSE ISLAND	69284-4/$3.99
☐ #99: THE SECRET AT SEVEN ROCKS	69285-2/$3.99
☐ #100: A SECRET IN TIME	69286-0/$3.99
☐ #101: THE MYSTERY OF THE MISSING	69287-9/$3.99
MILLIONAIRES	
☐ #102: THE SECRET IN THE DARK	69279-8/$3.99
☐ #103: THE STRANGER IN THE SHADOWS	73049-5/$3.99
☐ #104: THE MYSTERY OF THE JADE TIGER	73050-9/$3.99
☐ #105: THE CLUE IN THE ANTIQUE TRUNK	73051-7/$3.99
☐ #106: THE CASE OF THE ARTFUL CRIME	73052-5/$3.99
☐ #107: THE LEGEND OF MINER'S CREEK	73053-3/$3.99
☐ #108: THE SECRET OF THE TIBETAN	73054-1/$3.99
TREASURE	
☐ #109: THE MYSTERY OF THE MASKED RIDER	73055-X/$3.99
☐ #110: THE NUTCRACKER BALLET MYSTERY	73056-8/$3.99
☐ #111: THE SECRET AT SOLAIRE	79297-0/$3.99
☐ #112: CRIME IN THE QUEEN'S COURT	79298-9/$3.99
☐ #113: THE SECRET LOST AT SEA	79299-7/$3.99
☐ NANCY DREW GHOST STORIES - #1	69132-5/$3.50